W9-AYM-907

Praise for
Antoine Volodine

"Clever and incisive."
—*New York Times*

"These wonderful stories fool around on
the frontiers of the imagination."
—Shelley Jackson

"His quirky and eccentric narrative achieves quite
staggering and electric effects. . . . Dazzling in its
epic proportions and imaginative scope."
—*The Nation*

"Volodine isn't afraid to tangle animate and inanimate spirits,
or thwart expectations. He delights in breaking down our
well-honed meters of what's supposed to happen."
—*Believer*

"His talent surfaces time and again in luxurious, hypnotic ways."
—*Publishers Weekly*

"*Minor Angels* has all the markings of a masterpiece:
compression, resonance, and vision."
—*Literary Review*

"Irreducible to any single literary genre, the Volodinian
cosmos is skillfully crafted, fusing elements of science fiction
with magical realism and political commentary."
—*Music & Literature*

Also in English by
Antoine Volodine
(a.k.a., Lutz Bassman & Manuela Draeger)

In the Time of the Blue Ball
Minor Angels
Naming the Jungle
Post-Exoticism in Ten Lessons, Lesson Eleven
We Monks and Soldiers
Writers

THE BRYANT LIBRARY
2 PAPER MILL ROAD
ROSLYN, NY 11576-

Bardo or Not Bardo

Antoine Volodine

OPEN LETTER
LITERARY TRANSLATIONS FROM THE UNIVERSITY OF ROCHESTER

Translated from
the French by
J. T. Mahany

Copyright © Éditions du Seuil, 2004
Translation copyright © 2016 by J. T. Mahany

First edition, 2016
All rights reserved

Library of Congress Cataloging-in-Publication Data: Available.
ISBN-13: 978-1-940953-33-5 / ISBN-10: 1-940953-33-2

Printed on acid-free paper in the United States of America.

Text set in Dante, a mid-20th-century book typeface designed by Giovanni Mardersteig.
The original type was cut by Charles Malin.

Design by N. J. Furl

Open Letter is the University of Rochester's nonprofit, literary translation press:
Lattimore Hall 411, Box 270082, Rochester, NY 14627

www.openletterbooks.org

Bardo or Not Bardo

I. LAST STAND BEFORE THE BARDO

The hens were chattering peacefully behind the wire fence, as usual, when the first gunshot rang out. Some of them shook their crests, others paused their graceless march, freezing a grayish leg off the ground, unable to make up their mind about stepping in grain and excrement, others still continued clucking blithely. Pistols were of no concern to them. Knives, yes, maybe, but Makarovs and Brownings, no. Then a second detonation rattled the quiet of the afternoon. Someone came running and collapsed against the henhouse's fence, whose structure was poorly suited to such a trial and so quickly deformed. The posts bent, a row of perches fell apart, and, this time, the whole brood of poultry was overcome with hysteria. The disorderly hens—mostly reds and whites, but two or three black ones as well—dispersed loudly. The injured man was clinging to the wire web. He wanted both to move forward and remain vertical, but that wasn't quite happening. He hobbled slantwise, indifferent to the cackling, primarily preoccupied with what sounded like approaching steps. His pursuer was catching up to him, a fast-walking man, preceded en route by a zigzagging hen, all helter-skelter, wing stumps akimbo. The killer reached the wounded man and wordlessly stared at him for an instant, as if he was wondering what he was doing there with a target that was already hit—quite hit, even—then he shot him a third time, barely even aiming, before setting off again and disappearing.

The target's name was Kominform.

Now, among the decreasingly agitated birds, there Kominform was, triply pierced and about to die. He was bleeding. He had been a revolutionary communist, he had demolished the henhouse when he fell, and, next to its bent-over door, he was bleeding.

No one had witnessed the execution, though it had taken place in an ordinarily rather lively locale, behind the library of a vast Lamaist monastery, where a century before, monks still practiced martial arts, and which today was dedicated to vegetable growing and farming. But, that afternoon, everyone was gathered elsewhere. Novices, lamas, and guests were currently sitting on the poorly-cleaned and not-very-comfortable cushions in the large prayer room situated in the north-western wing, opposite the vegetable garden, to participate in one of the year's most important ceremonies: the blessing of the Five Precious Perfumed Oils. A small summer breeze conveyed the calls of conches and the rings of gongs. There were also the echoes of collective prayers. At that distance, it was impossible to tell the sincere professions of faith from the routine.

The day was splendid.

For several seconds, the situation remained unchanged, then an old monk closed a door behind him somewhere in a corridor, came out through the back of the library, crossed through a patch of beans, and hurried toward the scene of the crime.

He was a hoary religious man, in a faded indigo robe. His body was wizened in its twilight years. He jogged toward the henhouse, as quick as his breath and his skinny nonagenarian legs would let him. Confined to the lavatory due to intestinal troubles, he wasn't able to make it to the ceremony. He had heard the detonations, and foreseeing some mishap hastily wiped and dressed himself, and now he was running.

As he often did, he was talking aloud, to both himself and hypothetical coreligionists.

"Hey!" he shouted. "There's bandits behind the library! Armed thugs! Come quick! They're shooting everywhere! They've hit someone!"

He went past the rows of beans, peas. Beyond that, the henhouse showed all the signs of irreversible disarray. The perches were knocked down. The sagging fence had given up the ghost. There were rents pointing toward the sky, half-pieces of slats, the top of the door. Everything swayed and creaked at the slightest movement. He had to get past a square meter of metal lace to see who was lying on the ground.

"Holy doggone!" the old man swore. "I know him! Kominform! They shot Kominform!"

He knelt down. Kominform's body was moaning in the scrapheap's grating noises. He let himself be manipulated, scrutinized. While he examined the wounds, the old monk gritted his remaining teeth. He kept his prognosis to himself.

His name was Drumbog.

Around Drumbog and Kominform, the hens were clucking, without a care in the world.

"Hey!" Drumbog shouted. "Get over here! The killers butchered Kominform!"

Nobody came.

"Everyone's over that way, for the Five Perfumes," said Drumbog. "The monastery's deserted. Nobody's in the library right now either . . . If I hadn't . . . If I hadn't had to hole up in the bathroom

. . . It's always that fermented milk . . . I can't digest it anymore, and I drink too much of it . . . How are you with fermented milk? Homemade Mongolian yogurt? Goddamn it causes some bad diarrhea!"

Kominform shifted.

"That you, Drumbog?" he asked without opening his eyes.

His dislocated voice didn't vibrate beyond his mouth. He couldn't be understood. He had a hiccup.

"He shot me in the stomach, the swine," he said.

"He's spitting up hemoglobin," said Drumbog, having neither noticed nor deciphered Kominform's mumbling. "It'd take a miracle for him to pull through."

"In the lungs," Kominform continued. "I'm going to die . . ."

"Kominform, can you hear me?" said Drumbog. "Can you hear me, little brother? Are you conscious?"

"I'm hurt," said Kominform. "They got me . . . Old colleagues of mine . . . Converts . . . They work for the mafia now, for the billionaires in power . . . Social democrats and the nouveau riche and the like . . . There's nothing worse than converts . . ."

The end of an iron wire had snagged the right sleeve of his coat and, whenever he tensed up a little to stammer, the fence started to creak. It was like someone writhing on a bad box-spring.

"Don't wear yourself out, little brother," suggested Drumbog. "Open your mouth. You have to let air find a passage through the blood."

"That you, Drumbog?" asked Kominform.

"Yes, little brother, it's me. I was on my way to the ceremony, the Five Precious Perfumed Oils, right? And all of a sudden I heard machine guns . . ."

"Don't worry about me," said Kominform. "Go. Don't miss the benediction. Go on. Leave me here."

His chest rose weakly.

He vomited blood.

The fence creaked.

"Anyway, I don't have long," he continued. "I'm done for."

He clenched his jaw and went quiet. He hadn't been an adherent to communism to show off, he hadn't defended its principles to one-up prisoners. This was not the kind of man to weep in the face of death.

At that moment, the shells of dry vegetables cracked on the trail, the grass hissed. A hen fled, shouting in its avian dialect, put out from just almost being kicked. Someone was approaching.

"Holy cow!" Drumbog swore. "The killers are coming back! They're going to liquidate any troublesome witnesses. Anyone would do the same in their place . . . It's my turn next, you'll see, I'm not going to cut it!"

His breath was short. A hint of sudden dread clutched his throat. The shrubs and folds in the fence hid the indignant hen from him, as well as the foot that had provoked its vehemence.

"In the past," he continued, "if an astrologer had told me that my fate was to end up full of bullet holes while up against a henhouse, with a revolutionary communist by my side, I would've laughed right in his face . . . But everything's connected . . . Cold yogurt, intestines . . . The blessing of the Five Oils . . . It was written . . ."

Whoever was walking down the path and stepping on beanstalks was now visible.

The surrounding atmosphere wasn't dramatic at all: the exhalations of summer, vegetables yellowing in the sun, gallinaceans enjoying themselves, pecking at the dust, grasshoppers, gong echoes.

"They're coming," the old man mumbled. "They're going to do me in . . . There's two of them, a man and a woman . . ."

There were two of them, indeed.

The man was holding a pistol and had the shifty look of a soldier who now works in real estate, complete with the ridiculous blue three-piece suit. Perfect for real estate or insider trading. Heavy and respectable.

It was obvious at a glance that the woman had no relation to him whatsoever. She was more of a bird than a human woman anyway, strictly speaking. Her skin was covered in a very fine layer of silvery feathers, her clothing a gray researcher's outfit. She moved with a dancer's suppleness, and, when she spoke, it was to herself, addressing a voice recorder. Her name, like mine, was Maria Henkel. She was there to describe reality, not to take part in it. She was pretty, with a scar on her left breast, a heart-shaped mark that was easily noticeable since her outfit was more than form fitting.

"We are behind the monastery," she said. "On the other side of the buildings, in the Temple of the Flaming Lotus, there is a ceremony underway in tribute to the Twelve Tutelary Divinities . . . Twelve or eleven . . . Perfumes are burned in their honor . . . Oils . . . A certain number are burned . . . Four or five, I think . . . They're either burned or blessed . . . No matter, that's not what we're interested in today . . . I am right now beneath the windows of the library, in immediate proximity to the henhouse against which Kominform has collapsed. That's what interests us."

Kominform was no longer vomiting. He still hadn't opened his eyes. He wasn't troubled by the vision of the angel-bodied woman or the killer dressed in commercial blue. He wheezed.

"He has been hit by three bullets," said Maria Henkel. "He is still lucid, but, in my opinion, he no longer knows it."

"Those two aren't with each other," Drumbog assessed loudly. "The woman's naked, she's pretty, she belongs to a different civilization than our own. She must be a researcher from another dream. Just the guy with the pistol is dangerous . . . What's the imbecile waiting for to shoot me? I'm ready . . . I don't believe in his existence or the woman's. Or mine . . . I'm ready to rejoin the luminous void which is the only indisputable reality . . . I shall remain tranquil, at the edge of things . . . indifferent to things, to their edge, to these people's absurd lives . . . I fear nothing, I fear absolutely nothing, I . . ."

His voice rasped. Even if you feel ready to take a bullet to the head, your voice might still fail you.

"Here we are with the three characters in this tragedy," Maria Henkel said.

First off, Kominform, alias Abram Schlumm or Tarchal Schlumm, a radical egalitarian, pursued by police worldwide ever since the world became exclusively capitalist, seeking asylum in the monastery of the Flaming Lotus. He is dressed in a soldier's coat from civil war years, his preferred outfit since forever. He's spitting up blood. He's going to die. His death rattle is audible, the chaos of his heartbeats is audible. An old, almost centenarian, monk is propping him up tenderly.

This old monk is Drumbog, a Buddhist who believes in nothing, save for the absolute equality of suffering between men . . . Equality in suffering, which is precisely the minimum program defended by Kominform . . . Without reserve, Drumbog appreciates Kominform, his discourse, his praxis. He is the one who pleaded the community of monks to welcome and hide the fugitive, when the question came up, eight years ago. Eight or nine. Or maybe ten. This detail doesn't interest us. Drumbog felt responsible for Kominform. He has also considered Kominform to be a bodhisattva, an enlightened man who has dedicated his existence to saving miserable humans, going into suffering to help the unenlightened free themselves from suffering.

Facing these two heroes, the wounded revolutionary and the Buddhist touched more by Alzheimer's than grace, stands a man, the one responsible for a special political cleansing team, set up after the regime change. His name was once Strohbusch. He had put an operation together with an eye to negotiate with Kominform, he desired to convince him to disclose sensitive information, he didn't want to liquidate Kominform, he had recommended to his agents to approach Kominform without violence. But his agents had disobeyed. One of them, a man named Batyrzian, had misinterpreted the orders. He was so excited at the idea of facing off against an incorruptible revolutionary, disconcerted by this contact with an underground hero, that he sent three bullets into Kominform's ribcage. And now, Kominform is soaked with blood, from head to foot, and is in no mood to divulge his secrets. The operation has been compromised. Strohbusch notes this waste, due to the barbaric inexperience of his men. He is sorry.

"I am sorry," said Strohbusch. "My agent must have thought Kominform was armed, that he was going to cause a ruckus, take hostages . . ."

"Are you the killers' boss?" Drumbog asked.

"Hey now," said Strohbusch. "Watch your language There was a mix-up. We never intended to gun him down like that. That's not how I roll. Or in any case I make sure it happens as little as possible. We're not killers."

Strohbusch paused. Drumbog was muttering disappointedly. He'd made an effort to receive death without panicking, but, ultimately, nothing happened.

"We could maybe try to save him?" Strohbusch proposed. "Your monastery must have a doctor, right? An infirmary?"

"I thought you'd come to finish him off," said Drumbog. "And then eliminate me."

"No," Strohbusch assured. "I came here to talk with Kominform. We knew each other, in the past. We used to work together, in the same organization. We have some things to discuss."

"His hands are starting to cool," said Drumbog. "His breath smells like a dying man's. It's over, he has nothing more to relay to the living. The butchers who killed him should just keep their mouths shut."

"What if you called a doctor?" asked Strohbusch, ignoring the old man's reproaches. "I'll stay by his side. You can go find an assistant, right? Or, I don't know, a doctor, an herbalist . . . Some kind of sorcerer . . . There must be sorcerers in your monastery, yeah? No? Or at least people who know how to apply bandages . . . Hmm?"

"The only useful thing we can do right now is to prepare him for his encounter with the Clear Light"

"Pardon?"

"Prepare him for his encounter with the Clear Light," Drumbog repeated. "Someone has to read the *Bardo Thödol* to him, near his ear."

Strohbusch made a funny face. It expressed incomprehension.

"Have you killers never heard of the *Bardo Thödol* before?" Drumbog asked. "It's a guide. You read it near one of the deceased to help them pass through the world of death, if they decide to wander foolishly through the Bardo until they reincarnate, or to help them liberate themselves and become Buddha, when their heart's pure enough."

"Wait," said Strohbusch.

He had just slid his pistol into its holster. His eyes were open wide, his small renegade eyes, which harbored an unconscious and trembling drop of nostalgia.

"You're wanting to read to him from that religious thingamajig while he's in pain? You want to read the *Bardo Thödol* to a non-Buddhist? A revolutionary proletarian?"

"Listen here, murderer!" Drumbog scolded. "Don't you dare try to tell me what to do. What do you know about this man? He gave everything, he kept nothing for himself . . . He spent his existence fighting for absolute equality, for the destitution of all, for brother- hood . . . He was vibrant with compassion . . . You know, religion aside, he was much closer to the Clear Light than our own monks who . . ."

Kominform gasped. His difficult breathing took effort. His heart's knocking sounded like an ill omen.

"Drumbog, brother," said Kominform. "Who are you talking to? Who's that beanpole above us?"

Strohbusch came to life. He was delighted to see Kominform able to talk, and thus hear.

"You can talk, Kominform?" he said. "It's me, Strohbusch, can you hear me? We were part of the same cell, twenty-five years ago . . . We worked with Services . . . In the Organization . . . Do you remember? With Grandmother . . . Remember Grandmother? Back in the Soviet Union . . . Remember the Soviet Union?"

"Leave him alone," Drumbog interrupted. "Keep out of this with your union and your cells! The time has come for him to detach himself from the world of illusions, he must now leave this theater of dishonesty to be dissolved . . . to rejoin the real world . . . where there is neither death nor the absence of death . . . I have to remind him of the *Bardo Thödol*'s instructions, while you're going on about some Grandmother . . ."

"One minute," insisted Strohbusch.

"Strohbusch is pushing the monk aside with his right hand," Maria Henkel began to describe. "He's pushing him without any particular brutality, but he has the physical power of a fifty-odd-year-old scoundrel, with which an old, nearly centenarian, man can't begin to compete. Drumbog's legs are caught in a patch of wire. He's lost his balance. He struggles pitifully."

Strohbusch leaned over Kominform, over his mouth dripping with blood, over his ears.

"Do you hear me, Kominform?" said Strohbusch. "It's me, Strohbusch, your commander . . . I was the one who had to activate you, when we had to . . . Back in the day . . . But then the walls came down, and we did too . . . Grandmother is dead . . . The world revolution has been postponed for two or three centuries . . . Or even four . . . We've dropped the glorious future like an old sock . . ."

The wounded man was regurgitating blood. Strohbusch bit his lips. Time was of the essence for his mission, too.

"Listen to me, Kominform," he said. "I am your hierarchical superior. You have to obey me. You need to give me the list of moles working for you. Names, aliases, addresses. We're deactivating the ring, do you understand? Well? Do you understand, Kominform? Your ring needs to be deactivated . . ."

"Leave him in peace, Strohbusch!" said the old monk, coming back to Kominform's side. "He doesn't belong to you anymore! He's already on his way to the Clear Light, far away from your moles and old socks! Go on, buzz off Strohbusch! I have urgent tasks to take care of."

The iron wires had started squealing mournfully again, since everyone was more or less moving around. Maria Henkel was dictating descriptions of reality in an undertone. She tilted her head toward her left shoulder, where her recording device must have been transplanted. The whiteness of her feathers was overwhelming, her seemingly-bare body could make anyone want to live, or, at least, dream that they would one day join her in her universe of uncertain, admirable birds. Her voice was lightly somber, sensual, incredibly hoarse. Kominform sat moaning nearby. Grasshoppers crackled or suddenly went catatonic in the grass, having been pecked to death by a voracious, red, and clucking hen. The sun was beating down. One part of Kominform's body was in the shade. In the distance, on the mountain route, a truck changed

speed, roared. In order to approach the diverse actors in the tragedy without risking touching them, Maria Henkel went into what
remained of the henhouse and stood behind an intact rectangle of
fencing.

"The dying one is sitting in the grass," she said, "leaning on and
seemingly entangled in the metallic material."

Strohbusch is squatting less than a meter away. Strohbusch
looks like an accountant right before his arrest for embezzlement,
he is pensive, breathless, he hesitates to act, he looks like a social
democrat on the night of a rigged election, he is uncomfortable,
he has stowed his pistol in his ridiculous jacket, he would like to
be less despised, he would like to be thought of as a good servant
of the State rather than a turncoat spy who's knocking off his old
comrades, a trickle of sweat shines on his left temple, he looks like
an prematurely retired executioner, he looks like a police officer
right after a critical blunder.

Drumbog, unafraid of being stained with blood, is busy with
the wounded one. He has just applied pressure to the arteries
in his neck. It's a technique many of the monks use to keep the
dying from losing consciousness. It is essential that those on the
threshold of death witness with full knowledge all the steps of
their departure. If he remains conscious, Kominform will seize the
opportunity before him, he will dedicate the last of his strength
to self-enlightenment and become Buddha, instead of mechanically
struggling to live and die again.

"Oh noble son, Kominform," Drumbog said, "you who in your
youth, before going underground, answered sometimes to the
name Abram Schlumm, and sometimes to Tarchal Schlumm, you
are enveloped in coldness, you feel oppressed, you see and hear me
less and less. The time of your death has come. Do not be frightened, you are not the first to meet death. Follow the example of
those who knew how to cope. Chase all fear from your thoughts.

Do not miss this exceptional opportunity to obtain the perfect state of being, and become Buddha, like all who . . ."

"The old man Drumbog is once again compressing Kominform's arteries," said Maria Henkel. "By his side, Strohbusch is tugging on the wounded man's sleeve. He wants to get his attention, he has some things to tell him."

"Listen to me, Kominform," he said. "It's me, Strohbusch: your commander. Grandmother is dead. All the underground networks have been deactivated, except for yours . . . They all have to be shut down, now . . . I'm going to take care of it, don't worry . . . Give me your list of contacts, I'll do the rest. I'll deal with them personally . . ."

"Drumbog," Kominform asked after wheezing, "who's that guy circling around us? I could've sworn he mentioned Strohbusch's name . . ."

He paused to vomit more blood. His pulse was in the sonic foreground. It remained there for several seconds, disordered and ominous. No one dared to speak. Strohbusch continued tugging on the wounded man's sleeve, but without using much strength.

"Strohbusch, yes . . ." Kominform continued after hiccupping. "I remember a Strohbusch. A ladder climber . . . With a weak spine . . . He must've repented like the others . . . switched sides . . . I wouldn't be shocked if he were a model social democrat now . . . Servicing any and every government around . . . He probably licks mafia men's boots . . . Grandmother should've eliminated him like she'd planned when . . ."

"Grandmother doesn't exist anymore!" Strohbusch pleaded. "No one's talking about the world revolution anymore, everyone's been retrained . . . in oil smuggling, in human rights, in the private sector, in war . . . Don't think about Grandmother anymore, Kominform. Forget Grandmother! Live in your own time!"

"That's enough, Strohbusch!" interfered Drumbog.

"Open your eyes, Kominform!" Strohbusch continued. "Earthly justice is dead! Give it up!"

"Enough, Strohbusch!" Drumbog thundered.

"The old man is using a tone so authoritarian that Strohbusch submits immediately," Maria Henkel remarked. "The special governmental cleansing-team leader lets go of Kominform's sleeve. He shakes his head. He is temporarily giving up on making Kominform speak. This is a man who concedes to authority, a man used to suffering humiliations in order to live in his time and stay in the race."

"He's going to die," said Drumbog. "This is an exemplary individual, unwavering in his sacrifice. A moral rock. Don't try to shake him, Strohbusch! People like him are one in a million . . ."

"Whatever," Strohbusch grumbled. "If you say so . . . But you know, back in the day, I myself . . ."

"Make yourself useful," said Drumbog, "instead of asinine. Help me. He can't lose consciousness. He needs to stay lucid for his confrontation with the Clear Light."

"I really don't see what I could do," Strohbusch objected.

"Someone has to keep him awake," said Drumbog. "By any means necessary. And, at the same time, someone has to recite the book to him, so he doesn't spend his last moments thinking about twaddle."

"I could work on the arteries, I could, I could keep pressure on them," Strohbusch proposed. "I saw how you were doing it earlier. If you want, I . . ."

"I used to know the book by heart," Drumbog cut him off. "I could recite the whole thing. Page by page, my entire *Bardo Thödol*. From the first line to the last. But my memory's not what it used to be. I need something in front of my eyes to remember . . ."

"Oh," said Strohbusch.

"Go on, Strohbusch! Make yourself useful! See the stairs over there? The first door on the left . . . It'll take you right to the reading room. No one will bother you. They're all somewhere else, praying."

"And what will I be doing in the reading room?" asked Strohbusch.

"You're going to find a copy of the *Bardo Thödol* and bring it back to me! Posthaste!"

Strohbusch got up. He danced from one foot to the other. He hadn't escaped the spatters when Kominform was coughing up blood, and now his suit was festooned with stains.

"It's just that I don't know how to read Tibetan," he said, confused. "How am I going to . . . In a strange new library, how am I supposed to find . . ."

"You'll find it," Drumbog assured him. "There's practically no chance at all you'll get it wrong. Let your intuition guide you . . . You'll know instantly when you see a book so profoundly connected with death . . . The title on the cover is in Tibetan, but the text itself is in a universal shamanic language . . . the language of the dead . . ."

"My intuition," Strohbusch repeated skeptically. "But I don't . . ."

"Don't what?" the old man asked, getting angry. "Why haven't you left yet? Hurry, yakdarnit! Run, Strohbusch!"

Maria Henkel took advantage of the situation to get out of the henhouse and go back to the tufts of dry grass that crackled in the sun. She felt more at ease on the small trail, it would seem, and, two steps away from Kominform, she had as complete a view of events as she did examining reality from behind the fence. Here she filled her lungs with more pleasant, less guano-laden, air. Her magnificent body was visibly pulsating. Her white suit censored no anatomical detail. The feathers on her face quivered as if there were a very light breeze blowing and carrying the echoes of bells and gongs. I had to fight the temptation to approach her, embrace her, or smile at her. Drumbog wasn't looking at her. He was

watching Kominform's reactions, since he desired above all else to
help Kominform become Buddha. That's why he wasn't looking
at Maria Henkel, despite the moving spectacle she offered. Maria
Henkel didn't take offense. She wasn't there to seduce anyone,
only to photograph the present reality in words.

"The sound of Strohbusch's quick steps," she said. "Kominform's death rattles. Echoes from drums, trumpets. Sometimes
collective prayers seemingly murmured by old men, though the
young also participate. Hens are scratching at the ground in the
vegetable garden. They have shining but inexpressive eyes. They're
killing grasshoppers, ladybugs, spiders. They're mutilating and eat-
ing them. The monk is preoccupied exclusively with Kominform.
He's bent over the hole-torn body, he's propping him up, he's
speaking to him. He feels he urgently needs to recite the first part
of the *Book of the Dead*, which contains directions for the dying. But
he can only remember choice fragments from the *Book of the Dead*,
disjointed phrases. The precise text has escaped his memory. He's
improvising while waiting for Strohbusch's return."

"Oh noble son," said Drumbog, "your vital force will very soon
pass through the nerve cluster in your bellybutton . . . You're losing blood, soon you'll lose your breath, too . . . A yellowish liquid
will start leaking out of various orifices in your corpse . . . I know
it's not going to be fun for you . . . Life is nothing but a series of
sorrows, death, too . . . It's no fun for anyone . . . You aren't the
first to go on this adventure . . . Don't fall asleep. You must stay
awake . . . You must remain conscious for everything happening to
you, from start to finish . . ."

"He's muddling through," said Maria Henkel.

"Think on the Clear Light," Drumbog said. "Don't let your
thoughts wander onto anything else. Focus on the idea of that
glow that will form before you, quick as a snap of the fingers . . ."

"Here's Strohbusch, back from the library," Maria Henkel announced.

Strohbusch had been quick. He had hurried, partly because he was used to carrying out orders as efficiently as possible, no matter what authority was giving them, but also because he was afraid Kominform had begun listing, in front of the wrong person, which is to say the nonagenarian monk, the names and addresses of the Bolshevik moles in his ring.

"Strohbusch is moving fast," said Maria Henkel. "He's stomping on vegetables like they're common couch grass. He's going out of his way to avoid tripping over a group of hens. One of them is swarthy. The hens are fleeing and cackling in irritation, in a cloud of dust. Hang on, Strohbusch has two books instead of just one."

"Give me that, Strohbusch," Drumbog said, grabbing the two volumes. "So you see, you found them."

"I hope my intuition didn't fail me. I hesitated a little. I took a second of the same type, in case the first wasn't . . ."

"For a moment, Strohbusch looks proud of himself," Maria Henkel commented. "He feigns anxiety, but he is full of himself. He's waiting for a compliment. And then, he notices that Drumbog is frozen in a sort of stupor."

"Is something wrong?" he asked worriedly.

"What did you . . ." Drumbog stuttered. "What is this, Strohbusch? *The Art of Preparing Dead Animals*, a cookbook . . . And this one, *Exquisite Corpses* . . . An anthology of surrealist aphorisms!"

"I warned you," said Strohbusch. "My intuition, I mean, I didn't . . . It didn't work . . . Sorry, it was a mistake . . ."

Drumbog's mouth was hanging open. He had let go of the books. He had let go of Kominform.

"Mistakes, along with disloyalty to communism, seem to be your specialty," he said.

Then he closed his mouth and twitched. He was now crossing his arms over his stomach. An intestinal cramp was making him twist oddly.

"Watch your mouth," Strohbusch threatened.

"Fine," Drumbog sighed. "Here's what we'll do. First of all, I need to excuse myself for a few minutes. I'm having digestive problems. Since I'm going back over there, I'll look for the *Thödol* myself. You, during this time, need to keep him awake."

"Okay," said Strohbusch. "Should I press on his jugular or his carotid?"

"Don't touch him," Drumbog said. "I hereby forbid it. No, lean over him and read the books you've brought. The corpses or the recipes, it doesn't matter. It'll hold his attention, that's better than nothing. Talk to him, Strohbusch, make some noise in his ear. His intellect must remain alert."

"Drumbog is getting up now," said Maria Henkel. "He's trotting off, bent over from stomach pain. Sounds of feet on the dry ground. The fence is creaking beneath Kominform's jolts as he vomits more blood."

Cluckings of hens.

Kominform's cardiac drum.

"Kominform, can you hear me?" asks Strohbusch. "Please don't pass out . . . The old man's gone to do his business, so you can speak in confidence . . . Say something, Kominform! Your commander commands it! Tell me the names of the moles who are still alive, who obey only you . . . Give me the passwords . . . Grandmother is dead, the revolution is dead . . ."

Kominform opened his eyes. It was the first time in a long time. He looked at Strohbusch, he closed his eyelids once more.

"Go fuck yourself, Strohbusch," he said, slurring his words. "Grandmother isn't dead, she's crossing the Bardo, at this very moment . . . She's going to be reborn . . . She doesn't believe in your existence . . . You're the demonic creatures in her hell . . . Grandmother's going to be reborn . . . She's going to reappear and sweep away your mafias, your millionaires, your know-it-alls . . ."

Kominform's voice broke. His breathing and speech turned into gurgles. Maria Henkel was squatting at his side to capture the sounds. Strohbusch caught sight of the woman now less than a meter away from him. He hadn't noticed her until then. He noted her beauty, the silvery, pure color of her feathers. Despite her questionable position and her suit's transparency, his gaze wasn't lecherous. One doesn't gaze upon birds with sexual desire, after all. Almost at the same second, she left his mind, as if she didn't exist, or like an object of the least importance.

"In the neighboring building, one can hear the sound of a toilet flushing," Maria Henkel whispered, leaning her head on her shoulder. "A copper cord swinging, immediate torrent, water hammer in a pipe. At the same moment, Kominform is pronouncing several indistinct words. Kominform is struggling to make himself intelligible."

"She's going to be reborn," Kominform said.

"Don't pass out," Strohbusch said, panicking. "You're forbidden from passing out, Kominform!"

"You're all fucked, you won't have a chance against Grandmother," Kominform babbled.

"Wait," said Strohbusch. "Don't be crazy. Focus. I'm going to read you some text like the old man said. Don't lose consciousness, okay?"

He picked up one of the two volumes abandoned in the grass. He would have liked to have the time to find an appropriate passage, but, since this was an emergency, he realized he had to read whatever came up without being picky. He opened the work and broke the spine, as people who are used to disposable books are wont to do.

"Listen to me carefully, Kominform. Concentrate on what you hear. Don't fall asleep. *The exquisite corpse will drink the new wine.* Whatever the old man said, I'm not sure about these kinds of sayings . . . Well anyway, think hard about what I'm going to read to you, Kominform . . . *Waking up harms one's core. Weasels eat cabbage and rations and cloves . . . To the last man, the committed musk ox through mistaken molasses . . .* Hey, Kominform, up here, don't pass out! *Sand smothers the world with gongs, rubbish, and hooks . . .* Don't leave us, Kominform! Can you hear me?"

"Is that you, Strohbusch?" Kominform asked.

"Oh, you're awake! I thought you'd blacked out . . ."

"I'm awake," said Kominform. "I can even repeat what you were saying near me, just now . . . Prophetic phrases, Strohbusch. *Taking up arms once more, we shall reestablish red passions in droves . . . To the last man, the communist must act to awaken the masses . . . Grandmother's world is going to punish your crooks . . .* The rest, I don't know . . . I . . ."

"I should never have read you these insanities," Strohbusch deplored.

"Strohbusch is throwing the exquisite corpses into a plantain bush," said Maria Henkel. "He's picking up the second volume. Inside the library, the flushing mechanism is worked impatiently. Then, through the little lavatory window, there's Drumbog's voice, severe, quavering, anxious."

"Continue, Strohbusch! I'm coming!" Drumbog shouted. "Keep him in a state of lucidity! Read him the books! Doesn't matter what! Maintain his perspicacity!"

"I'm doing my best!" Strohbusch shouted back at the lavatory window.

"Do better!" Drumbog ordered.

Drumbog's impotent anxiety was infectious. Strohbusch shrugged. He found Kominform's closeness to death extremely distressing. He was crushed by the weight of responsibility given to him. He cleared his throat.

"Strohbusch is once again approaching Kominform's ears, heedless of the bloodstains," Maria Henkel described. "He finds Kominform's closeness to death extremely distressing, he's almost forgotten what he wanted to get out of Kominform before the end, he suddenly feels invested with a sacred duty . . ."

"Listen to me, Kominform," he said. "Receive my words in the precious heart of your precious conscience. I'm going to read you the recipe on . . . Page 23. Recipe for old-style chicken. Listen to me, noble son. *Take some murdered chicken, preferably already plucked and eviscerated. Attack its cadaver, cut off the joints, slit the body with scissors, cut it up until you have ten or so unrecognizable pieces. You'll have to put these fleshbits in an oiled container and wait for the ruined muscles and epidermis to change color in the fire . . .*"

Strohbusch stopped reading. He didn't feel nauseated, but he inflated his cheeks and exhaled. He needed to make a comment.

"Do they actually want you to eat the chicken?" he protested. "They make it sound disgusting . . ."

"Keep reading!" Drumbog shouted from the lavatory. "His insight has to be keener than ever!"

"Strohbusch is continuing with his interrupted reading," Maria Henkel narrated. "He is talking to Kominform about bodily fragments that must be burnt, seared and caramelized dermis, dissolving fat, juices. The nearby hens are cackling, deaf to this depiction of their future. Kominform is mumbling a few unclear half-sentences. The sun is shining. The ceremony over yonder is in a phase of calm with little gong. Drumbog is flushing the toilet once more.

A door closes, the lavatory door, another opens, the library's, then slams. Drumbog reappears, he is now moving like a hurried nonagenarian, an enrobed nonagenarian. He is holding a grime-caked volume in his right hand."

"Here, see?" he said to Strohbusch, showing him the book. "It's not witchcraft, it's the *Bardo Thödol*."

Maria Henkel took a step to the side. She didn't want to be in the action's or actors' way.

"He's leaning over Kominform," she continued. "He's opening the book and, moving on, he's reading it."

"Oh noble son, Kominform, do not let yourself become distracted, stay awake, listen to what I am going to tell you. You are going to die, but you are neither the first to leave this world, nor the only one. Do not be weak, regret nothing. Your heart has always done the right thing. You have spread the idea of a strict equality between all men. You have striven to liberate everyone from the ridiculous ties that bind them to material goods, to material wealth, to the power it brings . . . Now, you yourself are going to carry out your program to its most luminous conclusion . . . You have the chance to liberate yourself completely, little brother, sever all ties, renounce individuality . . . I'm going to read you the instructions . . ."

"Grandmother's coming back," said Kominform.

He began to gasp and cough.

"It's a deplorable sight," Maria Henkel commented. "Kominform is having difficulty spitting out his words, they're stuck on his lips as a bubbly paste. The words are running down his chin, unintelligible, crimson . . . The dying man's cardiac rhythm has no more logic to it. His disorderly heart is fighting against death's invasion."

"Yes," said Kominform, in between death rattles. "Grandmother's going to come out of her sleep . . . She's going to rise up like a typhoon from nowhere . . . Strengthened by her experience in death she's going to rise up, it's certain now . . . The tattered ones will stand behind her . . . The poor have quadrupled in number since Grandmother . . . They're going to rise up and march . . . The rioters are going to swarm . . ."

"Do not fear what is approaching, Kominform," said Drumbog. "Look inside yourself for reasons to stay lucid."

"They'll be invincible," continued Kominform. "Everywhere they'll put inequality to the flame . . . They're going to build the kingdom of the poor . . . Finally everything on this planet will be shared, down to the last crumb . . ."

"Do not fear what is approaching, Kominform," said Drumbog. "Do not let yourself be overwhelmed by drowsiness or fear."

"I don't think he's listening to you," Strohbusch remarked. "His consciousness is giving out. In my opinion, he's just about to tumble into the void."

"He shouldn't be tumbling regardless!" Drumbog shouted, losing his cool. "He can't leave like an idiot, as if . . . as if he were sleeping! That'd be a disaster! He'd risk missing his meeting with the light!"

Strohbusch made an imprecise gesture.

"Strohbusch is making an imprecise gesture," said Maria Henkel. "He would like to push the moment of Kominform's death back, but he feels it's inevitable and very close. In his eyes, Drumbog has gone off on a meaningless flight of fancy. Kominform's beating heart is still audible, but it is weakening."

"He's dying," said Strohbusch. "There's nothing we can do."

"Help me, Strohbusch," said Drumbog. "We're going to find a way to sharpen his attention, we can't let him go out like this! Talk to him! Talk to him on your side, while I read the book into his left ear! We can't let his consciousness vanish!"

"What am I saying to him?" Strohbusch asked.

Both of them were panicking. They were shaking like there was
nothing more they could do. They stepped on the fence partially
wrapped around Kominform's body. The fence squealed.

"From the text! Speak from the text," Drumbog shouted. "Didn't
you bring some books? Open one and read!"

"Which one?" Strohbusch anguished. "The exquisite corpses or
the chicken recipes?"

"Doesn't matter!" said Drumbog. "Read them at random! Speak
solemnly so he thinks about death! But above all stop dilly-dally-
ing! Act, Strohbusch, speak!"

The wire fence was creaking less now. Everyone had found his
right place. Kominform's head was held up by the monk's arm, as if
the monk perched over him wanted to kiss him on the left cheek.
Very close to his right cheek, Strohbusch was speaking. Kominform's face no longer seemed to be suffering, he even looked to be
in a certain peace. He looked like he was sleeping.

Maria Henkel was slowly circling around the group to catch the
best parts, or at least a few details. She had an unreal presence as
a swan-colored researcher. She was superb under the sun, in the
summer light. No one paid her any heed.

"Now," Maria Henkel said, "Kominform's muscles have relaxed.
Kominform is beginning to wallow in his death. His breath can no
longer be heard, the sounds his heart is still producing are barely
distinguishable. In turns or together, Drumbog and Strohbusch
are addressing him. They would like him to contemplate the surrounding depths as he crosses over to the other side, tranquilly,
without vertigo."

Drumbog and Strohbusch are speaking into Kominform's ears,
each on one side, each in turn or together.

"Do not let yourself be overwhelmed by fear," the old monk
said. "Your journey is beginning, Kominform, but I shall guide you
through its first moments, and I shall guide you afterward, day

after day. Fear nothing. Do not regret leaving your loved and hurt ones behind, unable to bring them to the light. Others will come to carry out your task. Go in peace. Detach yourself now. The moment has come. Break from your memories. Prepare yourself to enter into a state in which you will be neither dead nor living. Rest assured, noble son, there is nothing terrible there. During your stay in the Bardo, you will have manifold opportunities to confront the Clear Light. Go toward the light, noble son, prepare yourself, starting now, to be confronted by it. Remember that only your fusion with the Clear Light will keep you from being reborn once again and from suffering."

"*The yellow bride makes bubbles,*" said Strohbusch. "I repeat: *The yellow bride makes bubbles . . . As you munch your salads the wild bird finds bloodpaths . . . The defaced suns buy the music box . . . The viola de gamba muddles the viola de gamba . . . Back from the harvest, the youngster's oldest girl chases our crawfish . . . Junks in pocket, you went back up June 27th Avenue, toward the wood stove . . .* I repeat: *Junks in pocket, you went back up June 27th Avenue, toward the wood stove . . . The three drowned men have enriched the silence of the vaults . . .*"

"Once you are in the presence of the Clear Light," said Drumbog, "do not draw back, do not take a millimeter of a step backward, think only of dissolving into it, go toward it and be dissolved in it without regret."

"*On Karelian dragonflies an artilleryman chooses the silt,*" said Strohbusch. "*If the love is gone the beautiful pianist will make her magical farmstead . . .* I repeat: *If the love is gone the beautiful pianist will make her magical farmstead . . .*"

They are speaking into Kominform's ears.

Even once his heart has stopped, they continue.

They continue speaking into Kominform's ears.

II. GLOUCHENKO

Brass horns. They can send a very deep note over an enormous distance, across the valley when there are mountains and a valley, when there is a rocky landscape, full of abrupt fractures and sparse grasses. That's what we hear first. Lamaist, Tibetan horns. That's how the book begins. It's an unusual sound, but one heeded without reserve. Straightaway we know that this vibration is a part of ordinary life and death. We like it immediately. It invades the world, the body's bones, flesh and images and even the dead mired in the body's folds, and it is soothing. That is what the first, the very first, sound is like. Soon after, a collective murmur arises. It spreads nearby, as if it were taking place within an assembly more interested in long prayers than anecdotes or pointless narrations. The voices are indecipherable. A ceremony is underway, in a language that does not seem to be our own. In any case, we understand it a bit less than our own.

Then comes a silence.

This happens several times: horns thunder, voices blend into an incomprehensible address, then comes a silence.

It's beautiful.

I then hear the voice of the soldier Glouchenko, and this music, these noises, diminish. Soon they stop entirely.

"Is someone there?" Glouchenko asks. "Did someone say something?" (Silence.) "What are those . . ."

He gropes around, an iron cup scrapes on a shelf and topples over into the void. It clatters violently against the ground.

"They've cut off the power, the bastards." (Silence.) "Hey! Is anyone there?"

No answer. Absolute darkness surrounds Glouchenko. So thick, so black, it feels like ink running through your fingers. Glouchenko doesn't dare move. He's never felt at ease in the dark, he's a little potbellied, not very skilled with his body, he's afraid of causing a disaster. He wipes his moist hands on his pants.

The chorus of murmurs picks back up. It'd be difficult to determine its point of origin, where in space. It is simply there, in the background to the dark. One voice is now detaching itself from the rest, becoming more distinct. The language hasn't changed: still more foreign than our own.

I don't think I can say I recognize this voice, since it has been depersonalized by the demands of the ritual, and flattened by its journey through the dark space. Despite all that, some of its inflections might remind me of something. A long time ago, I met a man who wished to dedicate himself to the exploration of magical universes. That man's name was Schmunck, like mine, with a different first name than my own, Baabar. My first name is Mario, but that's not important. Let's say that the voice I'm identifying here is Schmunck's. So as not to complicate the story, we'll say that I recognize it. It's a solemn, controlled voice, like those that frequently resonate in monastery meditation rooms.

"Oh noble son," the officiant says, "you who are named Glouchenko, the time has come for you to find the Way into the Light.
Your breathing has just ceased, your body has already begun to
cool. In the life you have left behind, you received a military education, since you were an artilleryman, but you also received a
religious education, long ago when you were infatuated with Buddhism. You spent several months in an ashram and were told many
times about the Clear Light. Now that you are currently neither
living nor dead, wandering through the Bardo, which is to say the
world that serves as a link between life and rebirth, you will come
into contact with the Clear Light.

"Come to your senses, noble son, you who are named Glouchenko. Remember the lessons the priests passed on to you. Prepare
yourself. I am here to help you. I am the monk speaking into your
cadaver's ear. I am going to guide you to your confrontation with
the Clear Light. You are now going to find yourself with a choice:
turn to enlightenment and become Buddha, like many brave souls
before you, or pursue the foolish and painful wandering of the living, who travel ceaselessly from birth to death, then from death to
rebirth, without consolation or respite . . ."

"What the . . ." Glouchenko says.

In the established silence, he cautiously advances two or three
steps. He has no landmarks, save for the iron cup that fell in front
of him earlier. The cup bumps against his foot. It gives him some
small confidence. He pushes it as he moves.

"There's a guy talking somewhere in the dark," he states.

The cup rolls. It slips out of his reach. He shuffles carefully
right and left, but can't find it. He's lost the cup. He stops walking.

"Hey, talking guy!" he shouts. "Show yourself! Did you turn
off the dorm lights? Well? I can't see a thing, it's darker than night
in here . . ." (Silence.) "And what's this cadaver business you keep
talking about? I heard you mention a cadaver. I'm not deaf. What's

with this cadaver and Clear Light business, huh?" (Silence.) "Hey, boys! Where'd you all go? Hey! Where'd you all go, you lousy . . ." (Silence.)

Glouchenko has come to a halt. He is not normally a cowardly sort, but he is disoriented, and afraid of bumping into an obstacle, or being swallowed by a hole again. By an ordinary hole or an abyss.

"Or maybe," he mutters, "there's been a short circuit, and the lazy slobs are pretending to sleep so they won't have to go down to the basement. Hey, guy who was talking a minute ago, would it kill you to go change the fuses? Are you pretending to be asleep now too?" (Silence.) "Fine. I get it. Glouchenko has to take care of it himself."

He starts walking again. If we listen, we can recreate his slow exploration of the dark. He collides with an obstacle. He lets out an exclamation of pain. He mutters.

"Dammit," he says. "You really can't see anything. Finding the meter's not going to be easy. There must be an electric meter near a door or in the basements. A circuit breaker. Gotta find a door, to start. A door or some stairs."

In the distance, the splendid lamaist horns sound out. The officiant's voice follows. It is suddenly clear and distinct, going straight into the skull as if it sprung directly from memory.

"Oh noble son, Glouchenko," says Schmunck. "I repeat this into your cadaver's ear, I will not stop repeating it over the next few days, before a photograph of you, or your clothes once your body has been taken away, or a chair in which you used to sit: the time has come for you to find the Way into the Light."

Schmunck's profound bass begins to grow weaker.

The speech is becoming an unintelligible rumination.

"I can't find a thing," Glouchenko complains. "No doors, no stairs . . ."

I suppose Glouchenko advances by groping at the space in front of him. That doesn't stop collisions. He bumps into things standing in his way that had gone undetected by his hands. Low pieces of furniture, stools-turned-nightstands. Sometimes he snags objects by accident. The objects fall and break.These incidents exasperate him.

"What is this place?" he grumbles. "The walls don't have windows. Those jerks must've moved me while I was sleeping. They took me out of the hospital dormitory, they moved me here, to this . . . I can't figure out what this place is . . . They must have waited for me to start snoring, I mean I am a pretty heavy sleeper . . . Good job, boys! That's a smart prank!" (Silence.) "Unbelievable how dark it is!" (Silence.) "They've been hiding somewhere the whole time . . . They're watching me, laughing quietly, those idiots . . ."

He shouts.

"So you think this is funny?"

I didn't respond, but, to tell the truth, I didn't think it was terribly funny. A little, certainly, but not terribly so. If I had had the chance to exchange a few words with Glouchenko, I would have preferred to reason with him without laughing in his face. I would have tried to make him admit that he was not the victim of a joke by his barrack mates, and that the situation was, at heart, much more serious. But, restricted to my role as an outside commentator, I had no way to make myself heard to him. Any communication between us was out of the question. I could certainly establish audible contacts, but not with him. Only with the manager of Studio One-Five-Zero-Nine. We spoke to each other over the radio when the waves transmitted.

I was on duty. I'm a reporter. I get sent to places my colleagues don't want to go, in general from fear of boredom rather than misfortune or death. I'm the youngest, so it's normal for me to get the drudgework. And now I've been assigned to report on the Bardo. I'm not complaining. The management decides where I'll go, and I obey. Everything must be explored, so that the radio public is not ignorant of any of the strange nooks and crannies in the world. On my professional license, there is my name, Mario Schmunck, followed by a mention of my grandiloquent way of thinking. Mario Schmunck, special correspondent. They could have simply written that I'm a journalist.

"Are you receiving me?" I said. "Hello, can you hear me? Am I on air?"

Before my departure, I'd been set up with a device in my ear, and another in my mouth, near my uvula, supposedly so it wouldn't get in the way. Communicating was a nuisance. It lacked power, parasites often made it inaudible. The Bardo is a part of the world, but wonders of technology don't work in it. Since I'd arrived, my wireless systems had been malfunctioning.

"Hello?" I repeated. "Studio One-Five-Zero-Nine, can you hear me?"

I got a response.

"Good," I said. "I'll start then. Four, three, two, one, hello. Mario Schmunck here, special envoy for the Off-Shore-Info Broadcast. I've been asked to do a report on what's going on here." (A pause.) "We are currently in the Bardo. What is the Bardo? It's not easy to define without resorting to complete nonsense. Since I'm addressing non-specialists, I'll simplify. Let's say that it's a world before life and after death. It's a floating state in which those who have just died awaken. A state or a world. Floating, either way."

A pause.

"At the moment, it's very dark," says Mario Schmunck. "There's neither up nor down, left nor right, nor any measurable flow of time. In any case, that's the first impression people have of it. People starting their walk through the Bardo." (A pause.) "Him,

for example. This man here, this freshly deceased man is named
Glouchenko. He can't see a thing. He's moving slowly, cautiously,
through the shadows, but he's a bit clumsy, and keeps bumping
into obstacles. He's already knocked over a stool, banged into a
crate serving as a nightstand. He destabilized a shelf with a swing
of his shoulder. He's basically blind. Now, he's heading toward
a military trunk heaped with utensils and tableware. He's going
right over it. He's going to trample it head-on."

The impact is violent. Some of the tableware is dashed to the
ground. The aluminum dishes bounce and roll away.

"Dammit dammit shit goddammit!" Glouchenko shouts.

Several fragile objects are in pieces. Vials, phials. Medical equipment. Glouchenko howls. He's hurt himself, the shadows annoy
him.

"He's back in the thick of it," Mario Schmunck comments. "He
hit his right knee and toppled over, his arms swinging through the
void. He's hurt. It'd be better if he just stood still, but the darkness
puts him on edge, so he's agitated. He hopes he can find the basement. He'd like to place his hand on a circuit breaker, flip a switch,
and get the power back on. So he started looking for a stairwell,
some sort of passage down to the cellar. He has hardly any doubts
about where he is. He's certain he's in a hospital dormitory or barracks. Barracks because he comes from a military universe, he was
a second-class artilleryman before his death, he'd been sent to the
equatorial front to civilize the Indian populations still hostile to
the market economy. A hospital because his life ended in a medical post . . . in a nameless village, invisible in the forest . . . Anyway. Moving on. This Glouchenko doesn't think for a second he's
nowhere, and that he's just begun his journey through the Bardo.
He's convinced there's a power outage. He doesn't understand that
he's dead."

Glouchenko makes his way through the scattered objects. Not incautiously, he shuffles his feet on the ground as he walks. He doesn't have shoes, he is wary of glass shards, he doesn't lift his legs. A metal plate accompanies him for a meter. He's not walking on a wood floor. In any case, there aren't any creaking boards.

"He doesn't understand that he's dead, no, not at all," Mario Schmunck insists. "Like most of us, such a thought doesn't even occur to him. The information has been given to him, however. He receives advice and explanations from a man speaking to him from the world of the living." (A pause.) "You know, it seems quite simple, from the outside looking in, to pay attention to what a monk is murmuring in your cadaver's ear. But in fact, no, it's not so simple. You keep on. You imagine you're in the dark, you're still alive, and you're the victim of a bad prank. You refuse to believe the evidence."

Glouchenko is obviously hesitating in the darkness. His steps are heavy. You can easily imagine his clumsy movements, his crude, almost animal, stature, his absence of grace.

"He's like a deaf man being serenaded with patience and compassion," Mario Schmunck comments. "This dead man, instead of preparing for his encounter with the Clear Light, is looking for a light switch! He keeps his hands on the wall as he walks, his only thought getting down to the basement. His name is Glouchenko, he is thirty-five years old, he led a normal life . . ."

Far away, the Tibetan horns trumpet anew, and, much closer, a gong tolls. It emits a melodious, prolonged note. A superb note. It would make anyone want to join a monastery to hear it again, at any hour, day or night.

During this time, the special correspondent consults his file on Glouchenko. He turns the pages of a spiral notebook. Details abound, like in a police dossier. Mario Schmunck came prepared.

"I'll summarize Glouchenko's life," Mario Schmunck announces.
"Primary school, professional school, military service . . ."

The paper swishes as the journalist wields it.

"I'm just going to skim through this," says Mario Schmunck.
"Obviously, I'll have to pass over some details . . . Delivery driver after the army . . . Buddhism attracts him momentarily . . .
He pursues an education in a lamasery for eleven months, as if
he were destined to become a monk, then gives it up . . . Often
changed jobs between twenty-two and twenty-five . . . Duck killer
on a duck farm . . . Gang of friends . . . Bad crowds . . . Dropout
laborers, subversive groups . . . Radical propaganda, egalitarist
speeches . . . Participates in a supposedly revolutionary heist . . .
Eight years of reeducation with a strict diet . . . Prisoner's medal
for an endurance competition . . . New gang of friends from the
camps . . . Social reintegration . . . Chicken killer on a chicken
farm . . . Then he forgets all that, he enlists in Auxiliary Forces
. . . He's sent to export democracy to an equatorial district . . . For-
ests, swamps, creeper vines, giant centipedes, malaria, Cocambo
Indians to subdue . . . In reality, he doesn't have the time to get
to know the country, or murder a single indigenous person. Just
arrived at base camp, he helps unload a seaplane . . . A supply-
crate explodes . . . Biological weapons, apparently . . . Glouchenko
catches a deadly plague . . . It was thought he had been vaccinated
before leaving, but he hadn't. And then, yesterday, he died . . ."
(A pause.) "A completely unremarkable life . . . Short, mediocre,
incoherent . . ."

I don't consider it useful to always say what I think, because it's
often shocking.

But I say this.

"A shit life," I say.

A pause. Distant horns.

Gong. Silence.

Gong.

Now, the one heard is the voice of the officiant, the voice of Baabar Schmunck, the lama. It never stopped, but we weren't paying attention for a while. And now, we hear it. The admirable vibration of the gong accompanies it.

"Oh Glouchenko," Schmunck says peacefully, "oh noble son, at one time in your past life, we gave you an elementary religious education. And even if you drifted away from us, after having been near to us, you cannot turn from the Way now. Remember what you learned." (Gong.) "Accept your dissolution into the Void and the Clear Light when the time comes. Renounce existence, consciousness, individuality." (Gong.) "If you do not, you will have to walk for forty-nine days, assailed by frightening visions, only to be reincarnated as an animal or human. A porcupine, for example, or a monkey." (Gong.) "A porcupine that sniffs stupidly or a howler monkey. For example." (Gong.) "Listen to my counsel, Glouchenko. Do not let your confused mind influence your decisions."

The voice fades. Schmunck continues speaking, but the stream of sound dies out.

"Do not turn away from the Path," the voice picks up again.

"Hey!" Glouchenko calls out. "Hey, you, talking guy! Where are you hiding?"

Glouchenko freezes. He cups an ear.

"Weird," he mutters. "Sometimes it's like he's yelling right next to me, and sometimes it's like he's whispering a hundred meters away . . . In either case, I can't figure out a single damn word he's . . ." (Pause.) "It's like I'm in a dream. That has to be it; I'm having a nightmare . . ." (Pause.) "Wait, what am I saying. If I were dreaming, I'd be seeing things . . . And there's nothing here. Only darkness . . . It's obvious that . . ."

He starts moving again. He extends his arms. With his hand or his foot, it's unknown, but he touches a telephone. One of those old models from the interwar years, with a round dial and fork, and a mechanical bell that jingles when you shake it.

"What's this? A phone!" Glouchenko is astonished. "I wonder if it still works?"

He shakes it.

"Sounds like it," he says.

He picks up the receiver. He gets a dial tone. He tries to use the device by feeling around. He mumbles. The bell jingles no matter what he does.

"Well, it's plugged in," Glouchenko notes. "If I could just dial a number . . . There must be a switchboard . . . It's usually zero-zero . . . Oh goddammit! How can you do anything when it's so . . . Is this hole a zero or a nine? I'll just try it, maybe . . ."

The dial turns, returns with a scrape to its original position, turns, returns with a scrape. From the device, after the tone, come the echoes of a tantric ceremony, skewed by minute electroacoustic disturbances. There are horns, conches, collective prayers, chimes, whispers. No distinct voice stands out.

"Hello, can you hear me?" Glouchenko shouts. "Glouchenko here. Is there anyone at the switchboard?" (Faint murmurs, less and less perceptible chimes. Everything fades away.) "No, they don't hear me. I got a wrong number, of course . . ."

He hangs up. Silence surrounds him. He doesn't know what to do.

"You bastards!" he suddenly screams. "Turn the lights back on right now! That's enough, it's over! This isn't funny anymore!" (A pause.) "Come on, boys! The joke's gone on long enough! Turn the power back on!"

A beat.

He picks the telephone back up. He listens to the dial tone. He slams the receiver down violently.

"Bastards!" he mutters.

Then we hear him take a seat next to the phone. He's made his decision. He sits, he gropes around, he pulls on the wire, he moves the jingling device. He places it against his leg.

He feels tired.

"Fine, might as well stay here and wait for someone to call me," he says. "I don't feel too good, I should rest for a bit. Later on, I'll untangle this wire, if I have time. The thing's all twisted . . ."

In the distance, an extreme distance, the gongs and horns cease. For several moments, there is absolutely no sound.

Then we are startled. With how intense the silence and darkness are, the officiant's voice takes us by surprise.

"Oh noble son, Glouchenko," the officiant articulates, "give yourself over to reason, do not believe what you see, the colors and forms around you are but pure illusion . . ."

Glouchenko doesn't react. He's heard nothing. *He* wasn't startled.

"Well," he mutters, "someone'll call me eventually." (A pause.) "Whoa, what's happening? I feel all washed out. I'm just completely tired, all of a sudden." (A pause.) "I'm going to wait for them to turn the lights back on. Until then, I'll just take a short nap."

"Oh Glouchenko," says Baabar Schmunck, "the skies now appear to you as a dark, navy blue, a divine blue light, marvelous and brilliant, springs forth in your direction. Do not be surprised by it, noble son." (Gong.) "Do not fear it, even if you are barely able to take in the view." (Gong.) "Place your faith in it." (Gong.) "This light is meant to welcome you. Just beside it throbs a drab white glow. Do not be drawn to it, for that is not the light of grace." (Gong.)

The voice is weak, solemn, pacifying, but comes from too far away. I mentioned before that I thought I recognized the voice as Schmunck's. I'm less sure of that now. I wouldn't swear on it. Besides, it's a detail that only concerns me and my memories, and

I'm not important here. Only Glouchenko here is important. Only Glouchenko here is at the center of the dark unknown.

"Do not be attached, noble son, do not be weak," exhorts the officiant's voice, whether or not that officiant is Baabar Schmunck. "Do not look at the white glow that does not hurt your eyes, look instead at the shining blue light that blinds you, look at it with a deep faith. Try to dissolve into its halo. Try to melt into the rainbow that . . ."

Schmunck, or a monk like Schmunck, starts describing the monochrome rainbow, and we would like to know more, but the voice slowly fades away. We would like to know more and we concentrate on the absence of sound, as if there were an explanation coming that would satisfy us. But silence reigns.

For a long moment, silence reigns.

Then the telephone's sudden ringing thunders through the void, strong, unquelled by the darkness, and, this time, it startles everyone.

Glouchenko has a spasm of alarm. He was dozing.

"Those lousy bastards!" he growls. "They're good at timing their shots! They don't even leave me alone during my nap!"

On the second ring, Glouchenko picks up.

"Hello?" says a clear voice.

"I'm listening," says Glouchenko, angry. "Glouchenko here. Who's on the line?"

"That you, Glouchenko? Can you hear me? It's me, Babloïev. Can you hear me? It's Babloïev on the line."

"Babloïev?" Glouchenko hesitates.

"Yes," says the other.

Glouchenko lets out a huge sigh.

"Stop kidding around, boys!" he says. "Babloïev went out with the munitions crate, the other day. When we were unloading the seaplane. He got messily strewn all over the water. You know that he . . . Why would you joke about the dead like that? That's not right . . . Why are you messing with Babloïev? He went back to camp in three different plastic bags, poor guy."

"Two," corrects the other.

A pause.

Since we are there as well, I explain that Babloïev and Glouchenko are sitting four or five meters away from each other. They don't see each other, they're using the telephone to talk, though in reality they could do perfectly fine without it. Their voices travel through the wire as electric pulses, but, at the same time, they traverse the open air in the short distance separating them. So we are in the presence of a blind, four-voiced dialogue. It's a trivial detail, but I explain it anyway.

Glouchenko grumbles.

"This isn't right," he says. "You ought to have even the smallest modicum of respect. Moving me to a different barrack isn't all that clever, but this is something else entirely. Stop mocking a dead man, boys. A dead hero slain in action."

"What are you talking about, Glouchenko? I'm right here, on the other end of the line. We're together. I saw you sleeping. I wanted to talk to you."

"It's a pretty good imitation," Glouchenko says. "It's really like it's him talking." (A beat.) "Listen, I'm sick of this darkness. It's gone on for hours now, so tell your friends that . . . (A beat.) No, there's no way you're Babloïev."

"Oh, come on, Glouchenko," Babloïev snaps, "it's like you don't even realize . . ."

"Huh?" says Glouchenko.

"Are you thick or what? Where do you think you are? Pull yourself together, Glouchenko! Look around you! Do you still not get it?"

"Get what?" Glouchenko is losing his patience. "Do you think

it's funny to talk to me like I'm the last idiot alive? I get very well
what's going on here, thank you very much. And what's going on
is that you've cut the power! So leave me alone!"

"Fine," says Babloïev. "I'll explain it to you. Both of us are dead.
Me, from the explosion. And you, from sickness. We're dead. Right
now we're floating in the Bardo."

A beat.

"In the what?" Glouchenko asks, calmer.

"The Bardo. The intermediary world. We're going to float and
walk around here for forty-nine days."

"Cut the crap," says Glouchenko. "You're barking up the wrong
tree if you think you can just jerk me around. You'll never get me
to believe anything you say . . . I can prove I'm not dead, because
. . ." (A pause.) "I would've noticed something like that . . ." (A
pause.) "So tell me, guy with Babloïev's voice! Was it you who cut
the power?"

"The power? What are you . . . Listen to me, Glouchenko.
There's no more power for you. No more light. You're dead, full
stop, that's all. There's no more light, or absence of light. That's
what it's like here. And it would serve you well to . . ."

"That's enough!" Glouchenko says. "If you want to scare someone, go find another victim! Babloïev or not, leave me alone!"

He slams the receiver onto its stand. The telephone jingles. The
communication is finished.

Exactly at the same moment, the echoes from the religious
ceremony return. Horns, gongs, buddhic mutterings. When they
reach our ears, they seem exhausted from their long journey.

Glouchenko perceives nothing.

"Those bastards are trying to scare me," he says between his
teeth. "It looks like they don't know who they're dealing with." (A
pause.) "Hey, boys! If you're looking for another gullible village

idiot, you're barking up the wrong tree!" (A beat.) "I'm going back to sleep."

A beat. He starts shouting again.

"Glouchenko's not the idiot you're looking for!" (A beat.) "I'm beat. The bastards've really worn me out."

Babloïev is no longer expressing his thoughts. Let's say that he's not on the other end of the line anymore. Let's say that he's not anywhere anymore. If everything is nothing but an illusion, Babloïev has no reason to continue communicating with Glouchenko.

"Since there's nothing to do here," Glouchenko announces, "besides sleeping and waiting for something to happen. If they hear me snoring, maybe they'll decide to stop fooling around."

He doesn't start snoring immediately, but he does doze off without delay.

He is surrounded by stray deep notes, murmurs he can't distinguish. The officiant's voice travels to him, but he doesn't hear that either.

"Oh noble son," says the voice, "soon you will be in the presence of a magnificent green light, an extremely rich emerald green, whose splendor cannot be described. Do not fear this light, take refuge in it. Renounce everything, do not be attached to what you still believe to be your memory or consciousness. Leave that behind, abandon it. Accept dissolution in this radiant green, join the light in which you will finally be no more . . . Do not hesitate, Glouchenko . . . The moment of your dissolution has come . . . Plunge into that light to extinguish yourself . . ."

A beat.

The voice is nothing more than a miniscule vibration. Then it vibrates no more.

Then, close by, the crackling of an acoustic system breaks the silence. Mario Schmunck is with us once more, and when I say us

I count myself as well, obviously. Mario Schmunck the special correspondent, the commentator, the journalist on a mission.

"Studio One-Five-Zero-Nine, do you copy?" asks Mario Schmunck.

I had returned to the scene, also known as the Bardo. I continued my report for the Off-Shore-Info Broadcast, and, after a break, I spoke once more from the intermediary world. The radio silence had lasted for just an instant, few listeners had noticed it, but, in Glouchenko's existence, two whole weeks had flown by. In my own, that is to say my existence, I don't know. I'm ignorant on the subject of which system of measurement I've been hooked up to since I started my broadcast. I possessed among my meager special-envoy equipment a glow-in-the-dark calendar to keep track of Glouchenko's time. Fifteen days had already passed for Glouchenko. But time was vaguer on my end. Was it fifteen days for me too? Or a few minutes? No one had told me before I left. I was about to ask about my union rights, and maybe even complain some, when management warned me that I was live on air. I swallowed my doubts, my demands. After all, the difference between days and minutes hardly mattered to my well-being.

"Mario Schmunck here," I said. "Ladies and gentlemen, listeners of Off-Shore-Info, thank you for tuning in. I am speaking to you once more from the Bardo, the floating world awaiting the deceased. Glouchenko is now about thirty-three days away from reincarnation. The shadows around him are atrociously thick. This is the stage on which Glouchenko performs. Hmm . . . perform? Actually, he's been moving much less now. He's less agitated. He's sitting next to the phone and spends most of his time sleeping. That's how his days have gone. Day fifteen . . . Sixteen . . . There's a stopwatch grafted to my wrist . . . Seventeen . . . The days pass . . ." (A beat.) "Not long ago, there was another guy nearby named Babloïev, an old army buddy. They'd occasionally talk to each other."

I got a call from the studio. I was being received poorly. I was asked to articulate better.

"Okay," I said. "I'll continue. Babloïev got in touch with Glouchenko over the telephone once or twice a day, but Glouchenko eventually couldn't bear Babloïev's explanations anymore. After a while he stopped answering." (A beat.) "Glouchenko is a typical dead person, all in all. Someone is trying to guide him, read him instructions, drown him in advice. And he remains deaf. He doesn't obey. So then someone arranges for him to have an interlocutor on his own level, a companion in the dark to dot all his i's . . . What a waste! He's a typical dead person, stubborn, narrowminded, dissatisfied with his lot, and, of course, unable to utilize the knowledge he received while alive. Even though he learned quite a lot about death when he was in the monastery! He was told about it day and night. But he . . ." (A beat.) "See, I have some ideas about Buddhism too . . . I've read the *Bardo Thödol*, like everyone else . . . Now, knowing exactly what I've retained . . . If I were suddenly in Glouchenko's place, I wonder if . . . Hello? Yes, is that you?" (A pause.) "Yes, okay."

I'd been interrupted by the head producer. He urged me to return, post haste, to my role as objective commentator. The states of my soul with regard to tantrism had nothing to do with my reporting. I was sent there to talk about Glouchenko, not myself.

"Okay," I said. "Got it. No personal commentary."

Silence.

Long silence.

The sound of a gong pierces the shadows.

"Day twenty-two on the control calendar," says Mario Schmunck. "Day twenty-three. The weeks are flying by. A limitless black thickness reigns here. Day twenty-four. Wait, there's that gong again. It's a safe bet that the officiant's voice is about to break through the shadows."

"Oh noble son!" resurfaces Schmunck's distant voice. "The soldiers carried your body away nearly a month ago, and I have sat every morning in front of a photograph of you to speak to you. I have addressed you with patience, while you have continued wandering through the Bardo like a frightened animal. You have continued walking aimlessly, as if you possessed neither intelligence nor intuition. You did not recognize the Clear Light when confronted with it. You have not benefited from my counsel . . ."

The voice, harmonious and convincing, weakens. The rebukes are non-stop, but lack power. It's a shame, because the intonation is really quite nice. Anyone would listen to it willingly for the simple musical pleasure. Glouchenko, for his part, understands nothing. From the start, he has remained unmoved. Schmunck's criticisms do not reach him.

"You are still locked in the heavy and painful chain of cause and effect," the voice continues. "It is high time that you liberate yourself, Glouchenko! Make an effort, Glouchenko!"

We hear a gong again, but the sound is so diminished there's no way of knowing whether or not we merely dreamed it.

"I'm going to stick to the facts," Mario Schmunck says. "Glouchenko is hunkered down a short distance away from the telephone. It is, let's see . . . My calendar is telling me that this is day twenty-nine. So, Glouchenko's been dead for four weeks already and still doesn't know it." (A beat.) "Between naps, he still believes the darkness is due to a power outage . . . He has truly closed off all other avenues of thought on the subject. He's waiting for his barrack mates to give up on their prank . . . From time to time, he wakes up and grumbles a few severe judgments about his army brothers. He might just stay in one place forever, dozing and muttering like an idiot . . ." (Distant gong.) "In *The Tibetan Book of the Dead*, the monks describe in detail the visions that assail every deceased person for forty-nine days, during the laborious crossing of the Bardo, but they didn't predict that Glouchenko would sleep near an old telephone, not walking, not going anywhere . . ."

Mario Schmunck has brought a copy of the *Book of the Dead* with him, just in case. Far be it from me to be the one to reproach him for it, mind you. I do the same thing too when I travel. I keep it in my bag. The *Bardo Thödol*. It's useful reading, an investment for the worst days. He flips through it.

"At every step," says Mario Schmunck, "before and during every trial, and also after, someone exhorts the dead to detach from the illusions of existence. You want to convince them to refuse reincarnation, pushing them toward permanent dissolution. You can't accept the notion that someone would want to live again as a conscious individual, that someone would desire to be reborn once more . . . to try their luck one more time . . . It's fine so long as you don't insult them . . . You get sarcastic because they keep trying to be reincarnated . . ." (A beat.) "In fact, I don't know if I'd be able to renounce that kind of prospect . . . Diluting yourself into nothingness doesn't seem all that appealing . . . And do you know how you yourself would react? In this situation, in the dark, in fear . . . What would you choose? Dissolution, or reincarnation? Nothing forever more, or a new life of suffering? For example in a frightening and despicable body? As a baboon, a chicken? A powerful mafioso?"

Strong audio feedback cuts through the space separating the inside of Mario Schmunck's mouth from the inside of his ear.

"That's true, I shouldn't have done that," the journalist admits as an aside. "Yes, I know, you've already warned me once. Yes. No subjective evaluations. It slipped out. Okay. No negative opinions about the system . . . No, I don't have any excuse. Okay. Won't happen again. Yes? A review for those who've just tuned in? No problem, I'm on it."

A beat.

"Off-Shore-Info, do you copy? Ladies and gentlemen, dear listeners, Mario Schmunck here. I'm back on air after a technical issue. For the people just now tuning in, I'm going to briefly list the steps of the journey the deceased follows, as they are written in the *Bardo Thödol*. Day one, blue light. Day two, white light. Day three, yellow light. Four, five, red, green." (Gong.) "Then, encounters with forty-two organized into groups of five pairs . . . The number is lopsided, yes, but since I'm not here to give my own personal opinions on the system, I . . . Fine. So. Day seven, encounter with the deities of Knowledge, armed with curved blades, brandishing skulls full of blood, drums and trumpets made of human femurs, flags of human skin." (Gong.) "From day eight to day fourteen, confrontation with the irritated, bloodthirsty divinities . . . And then, from day fifteen to forty-nine, wretched wandering in deep shadow, in great agony, through gusts of wind, hailstorms, and wailing mobs . . ."

Silence.

"At least," Mario Schmunck says, "such a scenario unfolds when the deceased makes his way through the Bardo, not when he sleeps soundly. Glouchenko's case is peculiar, I think . . . For him, it's already day . . . Pfff! Day forty-three of his nap . . ."

Silence.

Gong.

A not very strong strike of the gong, in reality, but, for some reason, this is the one that wakes Glouchenko. The soldier stirs. He yawns. He stretches.

"Wow," says Glouchenko. "I wonder how long I was asleep. Something like an hour or two. Or maybe just five minutes. Who knows!" (A pause.) "It's pretty quiet around here! Quiet, dark . . . No one else around . . . Although . . . Sometimes it's like someone's whispering in the dark. Must be coming from another building . . . Or maybe it's just a feeling . . ."

He stands back up. He stumbles as his feet find the telephone cord. The phone jingles for half a second and Glouchenko, by reflex, sits down and picks it up.

"Hello, Babloïev?" he says.

He rests the receiver on the cradle and starts muttering.

"Dammit," he mutters. "What's going on with me? Here I am talking to Babloïev, poor guy . . . Hardly disembarked, and already sent home in a plastic bag. No time to get used to the climate, to fight the enemy. It was our own weapons that exploded in his face . . . Talk about a waste! Those arsenal bastards, they'll pack things up any which way!" (A pause.) "Wait a second, what am I doing talking to a dead man? The darkness is getting into my head . . . The darkness, the stillness . . . I've got to move . . ."

He trips over metallic objects. Once again, he is walking into the inky night, his footsteps small and cautious.

"Nothing's changed at all," he says. "I have to go. I have to get out of here. I'm going to end up falling into a hole." (A pause.) "The room has to have a door, no one'll tell me different. I'll go straight ahead." (A pause.) "Go on, Glouchenko, you're going to get out of here. It's just a matter of minutes."

"Oh noble son," the officiant's voice suddenly says. "Six weeks have passed, and at no moment have you concentrated your mind on the means of your liberation." (Gong.) "You have roamed the shadows like a fearful beast, you have not taken advantage of the thousand opportunities before you to become Buddha . . ." (Gong.) "Now, it is too late, Glouchenko. You are going to live again." (Gong.) "Alas, Glouchenko, I am warning you, you are going to live again. Now, you are growing inexorably closer to your rebirth. You are going to be sucked up by a womb, you are going to be inserted into a fetus." (Gong.) "Listen to me, Glouchenko." (Gong.) "Try at least to have the intelligence not to enter the first womb you see, not to throw yourself into any available envelope, in order to avoid becoming an animal in your next existence." (Gong.) "Listen to me, noble son. I am going to guide you so that you choose a womb with discernment. A human womb."

"Hey, talker!" Glouchenko calls out. "Where are you?"

Glouchenko advances. His feet land heavily on the ground. The sound he makes, reminds us that he doesn't have to wear shoes.

"I'm sure there was a guy whispering somewhere . . ." (A pause.) "Hey! Whispering guy! Where are you hiding? Come on, greenhorn, show yourself, the jig is up!" (A pause.) "That you, Babloïev? That you, boys?"

He again advances two or three steps.

He has stubbed his toe on an iron mess kit or a grenade. He sends it rolling away. It bounces twice then wavers a moment, with an increasingly quick pendular movement, then settles.

"Listen to me well, Glouchenko," the officiant says.

Glouchenko has stopped. He listens to the sole moving object, which then subsides. Something in the air quality suddenly catches his attention.

"Huh," he remarks. "That's weird."

He sniffs.

"There's a smell now," he says. "That's new."

He's completely still so he can inhale better.

"Smells like cat piss," he says. "No, wait, not a cat . . . Or maybe a cougar . . ."

"Focus your attention, Glouchenko," says the officiant.

"It's wild animal piss," says Glouchenko.

He sniffs again.

"Damn!" he exclaims. "That's strong! That's really fucking strong!"

"Listen to me with all your strength, noble son," the officiant says." (Gong.) "Soon you will have been walking for seven weeks.

You are going to reach the journey's end." (Gong.) "Soon you will
see males and females in union. You will feel a deep sympathy for
them, a violent sympathy. You will be attracted to the notion of
quickly entering a seed." (Gong.) "You will want to be created by a
father and a mother." (Gong.) "Now focus your attention on what
I am saying, Glouchenko." (Gong.) "Do not let yourself be placed
in any random embryo. Act with discernment. If you give yourself
over to your sympathies or random chance, you risk being reincarnated as a miserable beast. You might wake up as a cockroach
or a snake, or even a yak, constantly soiled by its own dung. That
would be foolish, Glouchenko." (Gong.) "But all the same, you
were a human being in your past existence."

Glouchenko doesn't listen. He doesn't hear. He sniffs.

"It smells like musk," he says. "There must be stable nearby . . .
Hang on, no, what am I saying? It doesn't smell like horse . . . More
like a zoo, a bunch of wild beasts . . . Pfff! That's really fucking
strong!"

He gropes around. An indefinable object falls behind him and
breaks.

"Those imbeciles brought me to a zoo . . . They think they're
so funny . . . It just goes on and on . . . Their damn lousy joke's
gone on for hours now. Since last night, even, if I'm adding it up
right . . ." (A pause.) "Hey, morons! You think this is funny? Come
on, it's over now, cut it out! Turn the lights back on, now! You hear
me, boys?"

He cups his ear. Not the least response.

He then starts carefully examining the air again, bit by bit,
the dark air surrounding him, which is at present much hotter
and much more humid than it used to be. We hear horns, the
gong's moving resonance, but all that does not currently interest
Glouchenko. The smell of urine, on the other hand, mobilizes just

about every one of his senses. He uses it to guide his steps. It acts like a magnet to him. He is drawn to the trail, associating it with the end of darkness, associating it with life, liberty, and deliverance.

"Mario Schmunck here," the special correspondent subtly intervenes. "We were cut off. The station is telling me that the connection's been reestablished. So I am speaking to you once again, directly from the Bardo, on behalf of Studio One-Five-Zero-Nine." (A pause.) "The calendar shows that Glouchenko's journey is nearing its end. Glouchenko has been here for almost forty-nine days. He has inexorably moved toward the place and time of his rebirth. He has not listened to any advice, he has seen nothing, he has not been terrorized by whatever may be . . . To cross through the darkness, he has not ruminated on the ideas about death and the Clear Light that were given to him several years ago. He has not remembered the teaching he received, he has not counted on his instinct and his mediocre intelligence, and here is the result . . ." (A pause.) "Please note that I am not judging him. Since he was tired, why would he keep himself from sleeping? When I take his place some day, I sincerely don't know whether I myself . . . What I'm about to say isn't at all orthodox. But still, sleeping seems like a good way to escape the nightmares of the Bardo . . ." (A pause.) "Yes, right, that was a personal opinion. Yes, I should have kept it to myself, but . . . I promised, I know."

At the same moment, Glouchenko lets out a sigh.

"I'm dead tired," he says. "My legs are barely holding up. And my head, let me tell you . . . My brain feels like it's completely empty . . ."

He takes several steps.

A beat.

"Hey, it looks like there's a light over there," he says. "Straight ahead. Yes, there's a brighter line in the dark. Like the bottom of a door . . . I'll go that way . . . That's where the smells are coming from . . . It's getting sharper now . . ."

"At this very moment," says Mario Schmunck, "Glouchenko is moving toward the light he has glimpsed. He's groping around, his hand comes to rest on a knob. He's finally found a door. He pushes it open without any particular difficulty."

The door opens onto the night, a dark night. It's cloudy and starless, but the contrast between the night and the shadows whence Glouchenko comes is so great, everything appears distinct, as if it were high noon. Glouchenko rubs his eyes. The nocturnal light is painful. He is beneath immense trees, deep in a wet, warm forest. We see a lush landscape and, here and there, pairs of living beings. Glouchenko hears noises. He is a short distance from a couple of copulating monkeys. The noises belong to the midnight forest: tropical chirps and shouts in the background and, much closer, simian moans of love, the rustlings of leaves.

"Hey, you, over there!" Glouchenko calls. "What are you . . . Well, those two don't seem bothered . . . Hey! Were you the ones who cut the power earlier?"

Glouchenko observes the macaques for a moment. First with bawdy curiosity, then with a growing feeling of love. He likes these monkeys, he suddenly feels powerfully attracted to them. He is filled with the urgent desire to be their son.

The clamors and hot silences, the jingling of drops on black puddles, the monkeys' racket in the high branches, the dripping forest ambiance, the smells of wild beasts, of rotting wood, the mustiness of drey, the rasps of scales and chitin on everything, the vapors rising from the mud, the shrill grunts and juices of coitus, the odor of anthills. All of this surrounds Glouchenko.

"Glouchenko is approaching the sexually-joined monkeys," Mario Schmunck describes. "He is filled with the pressing desire to

be their son. He isn't afraid, even though the macaques are growing in size as he advances. The closer he gets to them, the more
steps he has to take to reach them . . . The couple now appears
gigantic to him . . . The male and female rise up before him like
mountains . . . He's drawn like a magnet to the womb . . . He's
walking toward it excitedly . . . He's still shrinking . . ."

A beat.

"He doesn't understand any of what's happening," continues
Mario Schmunck. "He now only has a single wish in his head: to
melt lovingly into these two beings, becoming a seed, their succes-
sor . . . All his memories have disappeared. He is afraid of nothing
. . . He doesn't realize how tiny he is . . ."

"Okay," says Glouchenko. "I'm going to rest here, while I wait.
I'll go in there."

"He has practically no awareness of what is happening," Mario
Schmunck comments. "We can just make him out in the fray."

A beat.

It is hot. It is midnight. The forest sways beneath darkening
clouds. Sometimes, for a second, the landscape is silent, but soon
the cries of monkeys return, the rustlings of plants, the drone of
selva cicadas.

"It's over," says Mario Schmunck. "I don't know if I'd have
behaved more intelligently, in his place. More gloriously. I don't
know."

I don't know either, and here, I am speaking in the name of
everyone.

We hear a brief electrical whirr.

"Yes, sorry," says Mario Schmunck. "I didn't realize I was still
on the air . . . No, of course, there won't be any more egocentric
asides . . . Okay . . ."

So, Glouchenko. Or what remains of him . . . He's going to lose
consciousness any second now." (A pause.) "That's it. The counter's

reached zero. Glouchenko has lost complete consciousness." (A pause.) "He exists no longer.

A pause.

He exists absolutely no longer. He's going to get to live again.

III. SCHLUMM

I was on a train; these things happen. I wasn't traveling for plea-sure. I had been entrusted with a task I had to carry out dur-ing the ride. An unpleasant task because it involved sending a man back into the nothingness whence he came forty-eight years before, like me, which is to say probably by mistake. It always sick-ens me a little to have to take out someone the same age as me and whose fate, deep down, could be compared from beginning to end with my own. I had been escorted until the last second and forced to climb into the car without any directions. It's one of our hierarchy's techniques, it rests on the conviction that, with each one of us perpetually lost in our own existence, there is no need to know where one is really going, especially when the vehicle in which one's work will be carried out is being driven by someone else. Nonetheless, since I had struggled in the last few instants, I was able to wring out a few images and give myself an idea of the path I would be taking. I had been put on an urban line, in a large city, let's say Hong Kong so as to say something and to respect the

principle of verisimilitude on which it is customary to lay every
narrative murmur. Let's say on the line going from Mongkok to
the sea. This line sees little use at certain hours. Clarifications can
be whispered here without causing harm to the Organization, and
even completely false clarifications always reassure the uncertain
who are listening.

The train was moving. I was slouched in the same direction.
Some claim that sitting in the opposite direction of one's journey
can cause serious physical distress. Until now I have never been
sick on a train, I mean from the car's lurching, or because I had
been bothered by dusty smells or bodily odors. Admittedly, I was
now having to travel under horrid conditions and in a state of
physical and mental disrepair beyond the ordinary, but the sickness had already broken out or been incubating before I got on
the train. In those days and nights, the mode of transport was
therefore not relevant. It seems that certain illnesses are terrible
when one travels. The bubonic plague, in particular, or beriberi, or
even myonecrosis. I'm only citing the most well-known afflictions,
obviously. In the case of short rides, the patient makes the best of
a bad situation, but, when the journey becomes interminable, the
symptoms are aggravated. Doctors have published on this, and not
the least known of them at that. In my case, I was suffering from
no major plague at that time. However, as soon as I took my place,
I turned my chest and face toward the front, as if, instinctively, my
body had dictated to me the best possible position to endure an
accident or misfortune.

There was nearly no one else in the compartment when I board-
ed in Mongkok, and, after something like a minute, the Chinese
passenger occupying the seat next to mine gathered her belongings
and vanished. My outfit is disturbing, I know. My old monastic
rags, which don't always get taken to the dry cleaner, provoke
negative reactions, aggravated by my preference for the squatting

position, at the foot of the bench, though it is a natural and quite comfortable position. I happen to be questioned soon after I've settled. I'm pushed back by the tip of a shoe sole, someone fidgets, my presence is deplored aloud. As I am serving on orders and the Organization takes care of me on my return, I tolerate these humiliations valiantly. I absorb the insults without responding and, when there are blows, I take the blows. Faithful to the Chinese culture of fearlessness, the passenger had not let out any unpleasant remarks before disappearing. Like our instructors say, you can still escape beatings and, in any case in China, there are people who know how to live and let live.

I remained like this, squatting and shunted and in relatively good health, from Mongkok Road to Cheungwong Road, dozing in the long, dull hours.

A little after Cheungwong Road, Schlumm came into the compartment. At this period in his existence, that he had a human form was difficult to argue. It is true he resembled me greatly, which didn't work in his favor. His destitute bonze rags stuck to his flesh and seemed to wrap right around his bones; it underscored the weird solidity of his frame and didn't encourage making his acquaintance. He passed by me, not glancing at me, examined the area around the window as if he'd discovered a place of utmost importance, where perhaps he would have to spend several years in ascetic catatonia, then, having set-upon a course of action, he withdrew into himself abruptly and squatted against the ventilation system. He squatted in the opposite direction. His scarves and the very dirty rags clothing him, indigo, blackish brown, and very dirty, started flying and flapping around him. He extended an arm toward the air conditioning switch and cut the power. The rags fell immediately. Once there was calm among the fabrics, silence reigned, if one can call the din of railway journeys silence. I dozed off again; this lasted an hour or two.

The scenery went by indistinctly behind the window. Cheung-wong Road's sights had given way to Kamlan Street's poorly maintained storefronts. My view of it was very fragmented, between two fits of sleep. I'd have to press my face against the window to get a better look. I had been avoiding the window area currently occupied by Schlumm. The window seat is often preferred, even if it sometimes means having to travel facing the wrong way, and thus risk falling ill. The passenger can see what's passing by and thus thinks he can determine where he's going. It alleviates his anxiety. However, when you think about it, the reference points you choose for yourself from external images are quite illusory. Illusory or unstable. Let's take a simple example. Kamlan Street's surroundings, for example, meld into Kamfong Street. Apartment buildings stand in similar upright positions; the same four-character wishes for happiness are above every door; the crowd's Asiatic faces are all equally beautiful and touching viewed from the rooftops; the people all dress the same way. That's why I prefer to stay near the ground when I want to gather reliable information. Near the ground, landmarks are fixed, whereas at window level, everything moves vertiginously. Near the ground, my geography relies on simple data, it's limited to the metallic structures that dock seats to the floor. I can clearly see details lacking in momentariness, some hardened gum here, four black hairs rolled into a loop there, and, further away, a puddle of dark-gray dust. If there is anything that clears away my anxiety, it's these modest elements, and the picturesque tread that doesn't fade between lulls. I take comfort in that rather than in fleeting visions of architecture or crowds. Whatever it may be, as the end of the afternoon approached, I felt like going and observing what could be seen behind the window's glass.

I rose, and, using my hands to keep myself from losing balance, I went toward the window. Twilight hadn't yet completely overtaken the world, but I moved blindly, like I often did, which is to

say without caring whether my eyelids were in an open or closed
position. Certain mystics in the Organization insist that moving
around by feel and while holding one's breath offers fewer risks
than other ways. Though I don't always agree with these enlightened men, I admit that I'm not indifferent to such recommenda-
tions. I had already made decent progress when I heard Schlumm
whine. My left foot was bearing down on a piece of his robe. I
stepped several centimeters to the side and mumbled apologies.

"I wanted to see what was outside," I explained.

"No reason to ignore what's inside," Schlumm said.

"Your robe was in the way," I said.

"What robe?" said Schlumm. "That's my skin."

"Oh," I said. "Sorry. I didn't see."

"Oh, you see?" Schlumm crowed in a sinister tone. "And yet,
it's inside."

"Oh, inside, outside," I said. "We're not going to quibble. For
the difference that . . ."

I turned my attention toward the scenery and stopped talking.
I made sure now to open my eyes wide. I had to grasp onto the
crossbar to keep from stamping on Schlumm's clothing or epidermis. The hour had changed, but the scenery had hardly done
so since Mongkok Road. We were still in the city, surrounded by
stalls set up on trestles, protected by canvas sheets and wall hang-
ings, and it was raining. Shopkeepers came and lit bare lamps that
exposed cheap trinkets, T-shirts, padded bras, pieces of burnished
duck in soy sauce, assortments of pirated records. I noted in passing the presence, at the top of the stack, of some of my favorite
Cantopop stars. I greedily scrutinized the market's hustle and bustle
for a quarter of an hour.

"Your name wouldn't happen to be Puffky, would it?" Schlumm
suddenly said, from down low, from his mouth exhaling words at
the height of my left knee.

"No," I said. "Puffky is dead. He was found on a mezzanine. With his blood, he had had time to write: *Schlumm did me in.*"

"That doesn't mean anything," said Schlumm. "Everyone does that now. It's in style."

"I've seen the photos," I said. "It was a bad death."

"Bunkum," Schlumm protested. "There aren't any illustrations like that in the Organization's journals."

"An independent journal," I explained.

"Oh," said Schlumm.

The evening thickened, then Schlumm asked me if I knew who he was.

"No," I said, "who are you?"

"Schlumm," he said. "Ingo Schlumm. You might've already come across that name in the Organization. I have namesakes. Some Schlumms are dedicated to theoretical research, others are attached to the Action branch. Others still are just schmucks. But let's cut to the chase. The Organization warned me that I was going to meet a certain Puffky."

"Puffky?" I repeated thoughtfully. "No clue."

"Yes," said Schlumm. "Someone like me, not yet dead, but indisputably cracked. I say cracked so as not to dramatize the diagnosis. A guy who's not yet dead, with identity problems. That could be you, right?"

"I don't know," I said. "Maybe. My name is of no importance."

"Fine," said Schlumm. "All in all, if any name works, nothing's stopping me from calling you Puffky."

"Whatever makes you happy," I said, then I frowned.

Switching off the air conditioning had caused a rise in temperature. With the exception of a pinkish, dying nightlight at the neighboring compartment's entrance, there was no functioning lamp in the train car. We were surrounded by the smells of siesta and mold. Inhabitable space, by which I mean the space we were inhabiting, was filled with mist, with damp condensation, with miasmas. My brownish rags, my indigo scarves, and my feet began exhaling pungent locker-room smells. My clothes needed wringing out. I remained stoically inert for an hour, then I started thinking that an action on my part would be justifiable and even desirable. Taking advantage of a moment of inattention on Schlumm's part, I hit, using one of my good toes, the air conditioning switch. The vent went off, the scarves began undulating and flapping around me and around Schlumm's head, as they had done at the start of the journey.

Outside, night prevailed, but, as we were passing through a new commercial zone, the darkness was pinpricked with garlands of white bulbs. There were numerous vendors sitting behind their merchandise, heads bent over bowls of instant soup. If it weren't raining so heavily, we would've been able to make out what the noodles were flavored with, fish or crab or spicy cuttlefish or sesame shrimp. A short while ago the rain had increased. It was crashing down in vertical sheets. There were hardly any drops on the window.

"Tungchoi," said Schlumm.

Strips of grimy cotton were fluttering in front of his lips, so his diction wasn't very good.

"Pardon?" I said.

"We must be on Tungchoi Street," said Schlumm. "We've been zigzagging instead of heading straight toward the sea."

"Possibly," I said.

"You know the Tungchoi Market?" Schlumm asked.

"Tungchoi Market?" I said.

"Yes. That's what it's called. Have you ever gone?"

"No," I said.

A minute passed, cadenced by the skin or fabric flapping around Schlumm's face.

"So this Puffky," I inquired, "did you have any accounts to settle with him?"

Schlumm didn't respond. I turned toward him, though until that point I had kept looking out the window. I lowered my head in his direction. Lifted by the ventilator, the pieces of tissue fluttered in front of his nose and occasionally slapped one of his eyelids, his forehead, his mouth. I know that some claim we look very similar, almost identical, but, in the shadow of the compartment, I felt no sympathy with Schlumm's mask, a scrawny boxer's, unkind and psychologically unstable.

"I'm telling you, I'm not Puffky," I said. "Let's stop joking around about this. My name's Schlumm too. Djonny Schlumm."

Schlumm didn't react, so I turned toward the outside world once more. The train had slowed down, its movements softened, then stopped, like we were at a red light. The silence had grown considerably. Schlumm and I were unmoving, nearly petrified in the darkness, existing only through words and shopkeepers' lights, through exterior wet flashes. The pinkish nightlight was far away from us, in another universe, inaccessible.

"A namesake even," I continued. "In the schmuck category, I suppose, in your classification."

Schlumm coughed. Who knows if he had fallen ill, traveling like this, in the opposite direction and next to the window. I'd heard talk about him, read reports on him, on his allergies and neuroses. I also knew he was doing research into the loss of individuality during the forty-nine days of death, the feeling of splitting in two that contaminates one's journey through the first few hells. The Organization had tolerated these blasphemous studies until a recent date, as long as he reported his results, but it no longer tolerated them now because he no longer shared his notebooks with anyone. Hence my job, my mission. His emaciated and brutal face was awash with rents. Schlumm's cheeks and even his skull,

whenever smacked by the blackish tatters, did not make happy
flesh sounds, but were instead reminiscent of an organism kept
alive despite its profound desire for extinction, despite its violent
attraction to a definitive and irreversible peace.

"I don't believe you, Puffky," Schlumm suddenly tensed, moving away from my right leg. "You've come here to eliminate me,
the Organization ordered you to extract the results of my research
from me and eliminate me."

"You're the one who crept in here, Schlumm," I retorted. "Don't
go making wild accusations about me now. Don't try to reverse our
roles. You're the one who just suddenly appeared in a car I'd been
traveling in for hours already, since Mongkok."

"Oh, you got on at Mongkok?" Schlumm asked.

"Yes."

"Me too," said Schlumm. "There was a woman. My presence
bothered her. She changed compartments."

"A Chinese woman?" I asked interestedly.

Schlumm shrugged his bony and solid shoulders, agreed with a
weak breath, and added nothing else.

The train set off again, the light must have turned green. I went
back to squatting forward. Getting agitated hadn't done me any
good, talking with Schlumm had rattled me all over. This was
causing me physical problems. I now had spurts of fever accompanied by shivers and cold sweats. My neck was sore. In my head I
started going through atypical illnesses I might have been exposed
to unknowingly. It's not unusual to find infected gobs of spit in
public transportation. I had avoided them until now, but I couldn't
be totally sure.

"Has anyone spit on you?" I asked.

"No," Schlumm said. "Not that I know of."

We went without making any significant sounds for several
hours. We were right next to each other, sitting in our own way,

at the foot of the bench, in the thick shadows, and, every now and then, I felt the ventilator's wind hit me, soon followed by noisy rumpled fabrics, and, on my neck, on my forehead, the rips in our two robes became entangled, twisted together, folded back, snaked and flapped around. The train's route zigzagged for a while between Pakpo Street and Hakpo Street, then made a beeline toward Yaumatei.

I was seized by a terrible feeling of weakness. I nodded off several times. In all likelihood, entire days and nights went by during my unconscious periods. People probably got on the train and then got off again, coming into the compartment and then leaving, all without my knowing. During one of these indistinct mornings, or at the start of one afternoon, Schlumm once again turned the air conditioning to zero, and the swishing fabrics around us died down.

"Three days ago, a Tibetan woman got on at Lee Yip Street," Schlumm said.

"Oh, a Tibetan," I said.

"A Tibetan woman from the Organization," Schlumm clarified.

"So?" I said.

"She left," said Schlumm, "a little before we got to Shek Lung Street. She was looking for a certain Puffky as well. The Organization's put her on your trail. Her task is to extract information from you."

"What kind," I asked.

"Something you didn't want to give, it would seem."

Sweat began streaming all over my body, springing up in dozens of places at the same time and quickly spreading to all my folds and smooth surfaces, bathing me from head to toe, chilling me. I shivered.

"Information," I sputtered. "Information about what."

"About the seven weeks following death," said Schlumm.

"Oh, there are many more than that," I said.

"She was just interested in the first seven," said Schlumm.

"And she's gone now?" I asked.

"Yes," said Schlumm. "As soon as . . ."

"As soon as what."

"As soon as you were done with your revelations," said Schlumm. "You were talking in your sleep, you know."

"I have no idea what I could have gone on about," I lied. "The first seven weeks. Why not the last seven, too, while she was at it?"

"She looked happy when she got off at Shek Lung Street," announced Schlumm.

"What could I possibly have said? You were there. You heard everything, since you were there. So what was I talking about?"

"I don't know," said Schlumm. "I was sleeping too. My health's been on the decline these days, if you must know. I can't fight against sleep and come out on top anymore, like in the past."

He looked disappointed, concerned, but I felt like he was mocking me and I got up to fight him, or at least hit him. He knew too much, and it was time to eliminate him. We grabbed hold of each other. Both of us were soaked in sweat and smelled horrible. Our state of extreme exhaustion slowed our movements.

I started trying to bash his face in.

"What did I say during this so-called nap, huh?" I croaked. "Will you tell me, yes or no?"

He swiftly got the upper hand. I had been informed that he knew close combat techniques, kempo and jiu-jitsu moves, but he made do with kneeing me in the chest and then, at a point when I was sure my rib cage had been smashed to bits, tipped me backward and rolled me under the opposite-facing bench, with the same ease as if I had been a bag of bones and sawdust.

We stared each other down for hours, wordlessly, while our adrenaline dissipated. The network of ribs fencing in my lungs had reconstructed, bruises had ceased swelling on what should be called my flesh, for lack of a better term. I was suffering more from fever than the consequences of battle. Sometimes I had difficulty breathing, sometimes I didn't. The train went by or through temples. The aroma of incense and smoke came in through the air ducts. So as not to founder in morosity by thinking exclusively about my conflicts with the Organization and its henchmen, I tried my hardest to imagine the pious chaos at the altars, and the devout waving fistfuls of thin, incandescent stems, praying to Guan Yin or bowing hangdoggedly before idols, calling out to ancestors, demons. I've always felt a keen sympathy toward these rites, even when they look absurd to observe, supposing that I might one day find myself in a situation where I'd be expected to display such demonstrations of piety.

By the end of the afternoon, my bouts of fever were spacing out. Outside, night was falling. We had reached, I think, the eastern end of Wingsing Lane. I still refused to investigate the exterior landscape to learn where we were in the world. Beside the disorder of my damaged and dirty clothes, I could see the ugly angle of my right elbow and, in the distance, a ball of black hair, some hamburger crumbs, a semi-circle traced by a shoe's sole in an oily stain. I compared all this to what was already in my memory. Dedicating myself to this mental activity made me feel less affected by the shame of defeat and less tormented by the train's jolts. The compartment indeed swayed relentlessly, which at present was upsetting both me and my stomach. Essential viscera might have also been damaged in the brawl, maybe. I watched Schlumm for a moment. The switched-off blower was no longer mangling his scarves or the top of his robe, which was now hanging in tatters, since I had yanked on it during our altercation. Schlumm didn't seem to want to fight again, or dress himself in a non-miserable fashion.

Once we were past Wingsing Lane, I put myself back into a sitting position, a meter away from him, my spine pressed against the same bench as his. We stayed like that until morning, in the darkness modestly pinkened by the neighboring car's nightlight, then dawn came. You could start to make out a new urban scene on the other side of the window. A corrugated metal shutter suddenly appeared, then vanished. It was lowered in front of an indistinct store. I had time to identify the very simple character meaning "ten thousand," but that got me nowhere.

"Woosung Street," Schlumm murmured.

Having sufficiently sulked, I decided to act as if nothing hostile had come between us. A hot humidity clung to the space we were cloistered in.

"Maybe we could turn the air conditioning back on," I suggested.

"I was going to," said Schlumm.

He stretched his hand out toward the control panel, but the system didn't start up. He moved the notched button several times, pushing it back and forth on the aluminum rectangle, between an improbable flame symbol and the drawing of an azure snowflake. Useless movements.

"It's borked," he summed up.

"I can hit the top of it," I proposed.

"If you wish," said Schlumm.

I started to crawl toward the electric panel. When I passed by him, Schlumm grimaced.

"Your robe?" I asked. "Your skin?"

"Say, Puffky, I'm starting to wonder if you didn't . . ." he whined.

"I didn't do it on purpose," I said.

"Thank goodness," he said.

I reached the controls and banged on them with what was left of my cartilage, my bones. I was very close to Schlumm. I took multiple precautions so as not to walk on him again. I was in precarious equilibrium. We were suffocating, both of us were dripping with sweat, enshrouded in fetid exhalations, and at the limit of exhaustion, as if an insidious infection had destroyed our invisible internal organs, and prolonged its ravages whenever we moved or spoke. I kept attacking the no-longer-communicative switch all day, along with the system itself, which remained inert. The joints of my fists had split open, a liquid was seeping between my fingers, unusual beads, not really amber colored, but comparable enough to what grasshoppers leak when they're captured and afraid. I stopped exerting myself, I clung to the window's ledge, the crossbar, I straight my back until I was nearly vertical. I felt like I was accomplishing heretofore unknown acrobatic feats. Outside, the atmosphere was gray. The glass was covered in a dense mist. With my dirty, wounded hands, I scribbled a few words onto the damp surface.

"What are you writing?" asked Schlumm.

"*Schlumm attacked me,*" I said.

"What," said Schlumm. "Why?"

"It's also in case the Organization sends investigators," I said.

"So, you should put *Schlumm did me in* instead," said Schlumm.

We stayed there contemplating this for some time.

"As long as the murder hasn't taken place, it'd be better not to write anything at all," Schlumm finally said. "You never know in advance who's going to kill you. You can anticipate it, but you can never be one-hundred percent sure."

"That's true, there is a margin of error," I said.

I cast a sidelong glance at Schlumm. Evening was falling, and in the already-triumphant darkness, his features pleased me less and less. It looked to me like the corner of his mouth was wrinkled in a way that could only be explained as malicious irony. This man talked about murder indifferently, he talked about it like only a murderer can. Something bored into my marrow cavities and shot

fear into my blood and, five minutes later, I moved away from the
window and Schlumm's withdrawn form, motionless and calm-
looking, but now very disturbing as well. He looked like he was
asleep. I couldn't rule out that he might be actually sleeping, or
that he was feigning drowsiness, or, and this is the worst hypoth-
esis, that he was doing both at the same time.

I moved while taking a thousand precautions so I wouldn't get
entangled in the trails of fabric extending from Schlumm's body. I
wanted to avoid bothering Schlumm or waking him. I got back to
my original place, where I had sat at the start of the journey, then,
since the distance between us still looked ridiculous to me, since
Schlumm had just to lean over and hold out his arm to grab me
and send me back into nothingness, I continued moving toward
the car's entrance, and crossed through it.

I crawled down the corridor. The single nightlight still working
was emitting slender rays to guide me. I had decided to go into the
neighboring compartment, where just this light was burning, so
as to assure myself of more decent survival conditions. It wasn't
a question of escaping the agents the Organization had ordered
against me, I didn't have that hope, but only to gain some time and
space. In the unsupple night, its temperature the only warmth, I
fixed my eyes on that faded lilac, wilted fuchsia lamp, which had
become my pathetic star of continuation. I use continuation here to
mean everything that allowed me to avoid immediate aggression,
and thus still keep myself, for the moment, away from the termi-
nal void. From time to time, I made myself go completely rigid, so
as to hear whether or not the killer was on my heels.

In reality, I didn't perceive anything truly nerve-racking.

In reality, I didn't perceive anything truly nerve-racking. The
train continued on its route toward the sea, the wheels swallowed
the ruptures between the rails without complaint, the shock
absorbers grated regularly. The whistlings of air and iron striated

the shadows in a clearly not-infrequent way. My body escaped me a little, I felt like it was prowling and crawling around beyond me, already unable to fight against stiffness and fear, but the notion of not having fully perished yet had drilled into and stimulated me. Rather than gruesomely collapsing, I lifted my head. I braced my limbs toward the lamp and continued my progression.

Hours passed. I didn't stop for one second, even when I felt faint. I had finally reached the haven I had dreamed of, and which had been designed to seat about eight living people. The benches were softly brushed by the nightlight's rays. Tonight seemed denser here than elsewhere, most likely because my eyesight had diminished. Staying on my guard, I settled in as well as I could, at the base of one of the seats, facing frontward.

I spread pieces of my robe in tentacles around me, so the pain would warn me if someone were creeping up on me in the dark. It's a technique the Organization teaches to monks in the Action branch. It reassured me to know that no one could covertly slip into my life and remove me from it, however deep the shadows surrounding me. The Action branch's instructions also specified, for better security, that one had to abstain from making any kind of noise, such as breathing or other things. I kept myself from breathing, concentrating on thinking about the journey rather than oxygen.

The train was no longer moving. In the distance a loudspeaker was making an announcement. I tried to listen. The acoustics outside were bad. I thought I caught, however, that the next stop would be the Haufook Street station. So we were still far from the sea. Doors slammed in another car. Everything around me was now silent. There was no one behind the partition.

An hour flaked away, then the train started up again. The darkness, the soothing movements, the state of profound extenuation I found myself in were all right for me. Though I can't affirm it with certainty, I think I lost consciousness for a night or two, since, soon after, the compartment was filled with morning's glow. It sneaked in gently through the droplets covering the opaque window. I attentively examined the surrounding visible world. My memory was scrambled, my mind impotent. I saw things without coming to conclusions about them. For example, there were, beneath the bench facing me, a piece of hardened gum and several hairs, but I couldn't say if they were familiar to me or not. In the mist, someone had written in a clumsy and soiled hand: *Puffky did me in*. I remained there, before these humble pieces of information, trying to connect them to build a coherent intellectual edifice, but my thoughts didn't click. I wasn't building anything. I had a single constructive obsession, I continuously made sure I was still sitting facing forward.

From the other side of the partition, I thought I heard snoring, then everything that could have had a connection to life or sleep went quiet.

"Are you there Puffky?" I shouted.

There was no response. I waited a moment, then repeated my question.

"Come on, I know you're there," I said.

I started tapping on the partition to make contact between us.

"There was a murder," I said. "Are you alive?" I asked.

I continued knocking on the bench's supports, on the air conditioner's grill, with my right fist, my feet.

"Listen, Puffky, don't stay over there in your corner, I'm not going to hurt you," I said.

Puffky didn't respond, and, for several days, while we made our way to the sea, I had no idea if a murder had taken place or not.

IV. THE BARDO OF THE MEDUSA

During the summer of 1342, over the span of three days, the writer and actor Bogdan Schlumm approached the Bardo three times, under difficult conditions, without assistance. He could be heard reciting the *Bardo Thödol* in a powerful voice, then mumbling and, at the same time, pretending not to understand what his lips were proclaiming, and even feigning deafness. Three times thus he balanced himself across the Bardo's narrow passageways, a very short distance away from the black space, staggering between death and reality. It was a grueling experience. At different moments during the trance, he spoke like one of the living, or listened and expressed himself like one of the dead. He didn't move much, limiting his surface area to a few square meters of fallen leaves, already yellow, mainly birch. Atmospheric conditions were mediocre, which didn't simplify his task. The ground was soggy and it was raining. When it wasn't raining, an abnormal quantity of starlings descended onto the branches above Schlumm and chattered noisily, all while defecating on him, though sometimes they were magpies with their unbearable yapping. Nature had never been kind to Schlumm. Despite it all, he tried to make the best of a bad situation. He pretended to despise the adversity and guano, like the specialists recommended he do in this kind of scenario. He tried to concentrate firstly on his text and the gestures he had to make to better inhabit his characters. From time to time, he opened his eyes, his author's eyes, then he closed them again. He was very lonely and it was wearing him out. Around him, under the trees, there was no one to applaud him.

It was Tuesday, then Wednesday, then it was Thursday.

The absence of spectators was a phenomenon with which Schlumm had always coexisted peacefully, but, this time, it affected his mood, since he'd made an effort to get people to come. One week earlier, he had launched a genuine publicity campaign. Though not a grand strategist in the art of media announcements, he knew about some hypnosis techniques that were used on the masses, and had wanted to utilize them to attract plenty of bodies to his theater. He had written some agitprop material in which he specified the times of the spectacle and the titles of the three plays he planned on interpreting. Admittedly, he had forgotten to mention the dates of the event, but that didn't matter much. He had hand-copied the original agitorial text several times, which had required an enormous expenditure of energy. The finished pile was impressive. Without exaggerating, I think I can say there were eighteen or even nineteen identical—within a comma or two, anyway—copies. Bogdan Schlumm saved one of them for his archives and threw the others out his dormitory window. He thus proceeded with his first strike.

The papers flew. It was ten o'clock at night. The day hadn't quite faded away yet. Finally, it was gone. The next day, in the grass and the currant bushes growing outside the Zenfl Wing, Schlumm could only find eleven tracts. The others had been carried off by the wind, but also, doubtlessly, by interested people or Untermenschen. Schlumm felt encouraged by the results of this first strike and quickly came up with a second. His target was still the inhabitants of the Zenfl Wing, where his dramaturgical existence had already been remarked upon by the care staff, and where the idle and curious abounded. Standing near the currant bushes, sunk to his ankles in loose earth, he rolled the tracts between his hands until they were perfectly-shaped pellets. The night and the rain had caused the paper to gain weight and, for aerodynamic reasons, he couldn't reuse the pages as they were. The eleven tracts were once again thrown through the dormitory window, this time from the outside in. Four or five pellets rolled under beds and were lost, others didn't reach the inside of the building, fell back into the bushes, and were torn to irredeemable pieces. But the information had circulated, undeniably. And rumor was going to be born and make waves, first in the Zenfl Wing, and then in other parts of the camp. The grapevine was going to work wonders. All that week, Schlumm let his mad hopes grow. He fantasized about the audience to come.

Hence his bitterness, hence his great bitterness.

During the spectacle, like I said, Schlumm sometimes closed his eyes, and sometimes opened them. When he lifted his eyelids and succeeded in sending his gaze beyond his dramatized worlds, the images he received included birch trunks, plants, puddles, and earth. There was nothing else among the unmoving silhouettes. The public hadn't come. That Tuesday, that Wednesday, and that Thursday, neither fanatics of post-exotic theater, nor lost hikers, nor even other forest mammals witnessed the performances that Schlumm had so blatantly advertised.

In the public's defense, it must be said that the theater's location was only accessible by a long trek through the woods, the last few kilometers being a series of increasingly-muddy passages.

The choosing of this marginal scene had been dictated by ideological considerations as much as Schlumm's harsh schizophrenic timidity. No one had questioned him about it, but if they had, he would have once more proclaimed his refusal of official literatures and the facilities from which they benefit in exchange for their complicity. Schlumm hated the star system and didn't want to be ground up in that machine, such as by performing in a more traditional setting, like the Zenfl Wing's inner courtyard, or the canteen, or the offices reserved for the care staff. Moreover, Schlumm thought that the depths of the forest would allow him to explore his art without concession, far from the snobberies and prejudices of urban centers, zoos, or camps.

Schlumm left for the forest; he reached the miniscule stage, surrounded by silvery trunks and silence, an ideal spot for a post-exotic trance, nearly as favorable for shamanism as a cell in a high-security sector. He unloaded his meager equipment and, once the woodland scene no longer resembled a woodland scene, he began his vertiginous dance with the Bardo before death and the Bardo after death. He created spoken silence, to borrow a term he liked to use to qualify his theater. Then, when the spectacle was over, he packed up his belongings, ate an apple, and returned to the Zenfl Wing—which is to say his home, which is to say our home—to sleep.

The rain fell on the first day in violent showers, but after that the weather, however fickle, was no longer unfavorable for Schlumm. If there were any incidents, they weren't due to meteorological malice, but instead to the fact that the trees were laden with birds whose stridencies often came into direct competition with the actor's numerous voices, and whose intermittent evacuations interrupted or humiliated him. Even though he considered himself an Untermensch, Schlumm hated getting excrement on his face. He would have liked to keep going and not stop, but he always failed. The droppings were acidic. When they fell into his eyes or mouth, he had to wipe them away completely before he could continue experiencing his text.

Bogdan Schlumm played every role himself; he hadn't had the chance to get a troupe together. Of the three actors he had considered, one was in a state of depression much too intense to memorize a monologue or even stand mutely against a tree trunk somewhere, the second had been shot for trying to escape, and the third, after several consultations with the care staff, had made it known to Schlumm that he had engagements elsewhere and would not be available this season, or any of the following. Schlumm had thus decided to say and do everything himself, as usual.

The pieces on display, in the presence of obscure beetles and waterlogged trees, belong to an ensemble named *The Seven Bardic Playlets*, which Bogdan Schlumm also called *The Bardo of the Medusa*, to allude to the gelatinous nature of the voices and characters introduced. Bogdan Schlumm has always held that these scenes must be performed simultaneously, on a stage likely to welcome all seven settings and groups of actors at the same time. To the best of my knowledge, no theater company has ever performed *The Bardo of the Medusa* and followed the author's extremist instructions. There have been many aberrations staged in the realm of experimental theater, some of them reproducing carceral reality with a sickening minimalism, some of them dangerous for both the actors and the audience, others revolting, others still quite simply ridiculous, but that particular aberration has never reared its head. Nowhere in the camp or the world have Bogdan Schlumm's seven sketches been depicted fully and simultaneously. At one point during his stay in the Zenfl Wing, he tried his hardest to make us believe that a troupe of amateurs in Singapore, the "Baba and Nyonya Theater," staged regularly, on every second Sunday in November, the *Seven Bardic Playlets* in their most radical polyphonic form.

According to Bogdan Schlumm, the Asiatic audience came all the way from Sydney, Hong Kong, and Nagasaki to see these performances, with the same enthusiasm that pushes fanatics of Chinese opera to travel the globe to witness in totality the fifty-five acts of *The Peony Pavilion*. Upon inquiry, the Singapore story reflects Schlumm's repressed desires, his risible dreams of large-scale glory, in complete contradiction to his hostility toward the star system. In reality, Schlumm shamelessly exaggerated the facts. The "Baba and Nyonya Theater" had put on *one* bardic play *one* time, *Last Stand Before the Bardo*. The room had remained empty from start to finish, so the actors decided to cancel the second showing, scheduled for the following day.

Over the course of those much-vaunted days in the summer of 1342, the three sketches from *The Bardo of the Medusa* were also not performed simultaneously. By taking on exhausting feats of acrobatics, Schlumm could play multiple characters at the same time, but he had neither the strength nor the technical prowess to perform all three plays at once. So he put them on in succession.

Tuesday was dedicated to *No Objective*, whose theme is impossible scientific exploration of the Bardo. Despite the heavy precipitation, the text was spoken without any sort of interruption, and entirely through a long, improvised, very striking pantomime, revealing Borschem, neither dead nor living, nor even living-dead, suffering from asphyxia and despair inside the Bardo instead of returning to the room where the monks who organized the fatal dive are waiting for him.

On Wednesday, Bogdan Schlumm performed *The Coal Company*, a short, sober play, whose dramatic intensity he rendered with a delicate touch. The forest's natural decor didn't help his efforts to replicate the darkness of the mine, the terrifying darkness of imprisonment under rock after a firedamp explosion. At the moment when Schlumm emitted the two survivors' first breath, the sun was playing hide-and-seek between the birches and the clouds, coloring the stage with fantastic rays and making Bogdan Schlumm squint, undermining the credibility of his performance. Above him, the starlings spoke up. I've already talked about this plague. A flight of five-hundred individuals, at least, settled over Schlumm to discuss all their problems, passionately. They chirped, they whined, their racket didn't mesh at all with the enclosed, shadowy, tomb-like space where two unfortunate men were trapped, reciting the *Bardo Thödol* before the cadaver of one of their comrades, not really believing in Buddhist doctrine and slowly becoming jealous of the dead man. The birds made Schlumm's theatrical task excruciatingly difficult. Furthermore, as we've already bemoaned, they targeted Schlumm with their fecal matter. Schlumm clenched his teeth, but quickly lost his verve. He shortened replies or awkwardly dragged them out, all the while whistling and gesticulating to chase away the offending fowl. His head and shoulders were covered in guano. That Wednesday would not leave any major marks in the annals of bardic theatre.

On Thursday morning, new rainstorms arose, brief, gray. They dispersed the hordes of starlings. Afterward, a damp calm reigned in the forest, troubled, yes, by a company of magpies who for a few minutes threatened to reproduce above Schlumm the previous day's hell. Their cries were annoying, but the episode was short-lived. The magpies flew away and never returned. Bogdan Schlumm performed *Mishmash at the Morgue*, a humorous, somewhat-facetious bardic skit. His work as an actor was excellent that day, he may have even gotten his message across.

I have always regretted that only a handful of minor invertebrates, slugs or others, in general devoid of literary savvy, were witness to this brilliant performance.

Even though no one asked me to, I will put here, as an appendix, a summary of Bogdan Schlumm's three pieces. They can very easily be skipped over. No one listened to them, so no one has to go through the trouble of reading them; you can just skip over the pages and move on.

NO OBJECTIVE

The setting's cast is comprised of four voices:
Djonn Gavianiouk, monastery Superior
Wilson, monk
Meyerberh, monk, instructor
Borschembschôôschlumm, also known as Borschem, monk emeritus

Over these four voices are grafted, toward the end, a chorus of whispers.

The scene opens in a large underground gymnasium, its sole opening an armored entryway and, at the end, a hermetically-sealed oven door. The instructor's voice can be heard setting the pace for exercises. Springed machines are grating, a body is skipping rope, exerting itself, shadowboxing, or punching sandbags. The instructor is shouting things like: "That's enough, Borschem!" or "Stop breathing!" or "You don't need to breathe!"

The Superior has invited Wilson, an ordinary monk, to witness the last of Borschem's training before his departure. He explains to Wilson that he, Wilson, an individual of mediocre spiritual capacities, very bad at yoga, normally shouldn't be present in this secret room, situated well below the monastery's cellars. We're here, says Gavianiouk, in one of the Bardo's antechambers. The Superior was keen on getting Wilson to come so he could fill the role of naïve witness. Wilson's guileless remarks will be useful for the designers of the experiment. What is the experiment? Borschem is going to be sent into the Bardo beyond death, thanks to the particular training he's been subjected to for the past fifteen years, he's going to stay down there for three weeks, and then return to base.

Wilson is not at ease. He finds being so close to death distressing. He's frightened by the idea of Borschem's passing through what appears to be a boiler door. The Superior responds: it's just a simple corridor. Gavianiouk reminds him as well that he cannot break Borschem's concentration by calling out to him. Borschem was once a very close comrade, a sworn brother to Wilson, but he is excluded from addressing him, asking him anything or bidding him farewell.

In fact, Borschem's state is already different from that of the living. "His body is alive," says the Superior, "he moves and expresses himself, but, at the same time, he's right on the point of being elsewhere, so much so that he already looks like one of the deceased wandering through the Bardo, in the world after death."

Wilson has trouble recognizing the man sculpted "in dusty plastic," but he still feels a brotherly love for him. He worries around Gavianiouk. What will happen to Borschem when he returns to the land of the living? Won't he be forever traumatized by his journey? The Superior avoids the questions. The only thing that matters is for Borschem to report on objects and details, and that his dive furthers understanding of the Bardo, meager as it is at the time being.

Wilson approaches Borschem. He is undergoing one final transformation before his departure. He's stringing together extreme physical exercises while holding his breath, since he won't be breathing during his stay in the Bardo, scheduled to last a little over three weeks. He speaks breathlessly. He truly is a skilled monk, ready to endure the worst travel conditions imaginable. However, his conversation with his instructor Meyerberh has left him with a palpable anxiety. The experimenters plan to revive him on day twenty-nine of his journey. Fair enough. But what if time

in the Bardo doesn't line up with the land of the living? What will
happen, for example, if one day in the Bardo corresponds to half a
second in the monastery? Or, going the other way, if it's a month to
the living, or a year, or even longer?

Meyerberh reassures Borschem. He'll have a distress beacon on
him that he can fire if there's a problem. A tantric team will be
on-call night and day, ready to resuscitate him with special drums,
horns, and magic spells.

Neither the trainer's nor the Superior's explanations fully reassure Borschem, or Wilson. Meyerberh and Borschem review the
basic hypotheses for survival in the Bardo while Wilson, silenced
by Gavianiouk, looks on. He hears a suite of convincing-enough
instructions, such as: "If the darkness around me becomes unbearable, I'll close my eyes, I won't lose my good cheer, I'll move like
blood beneath the skin, I don't need light to know where I'm going,"
or "If a sea of fire envelops me, I'll close my eyes, I'll take refuge
in the rattling of my bones, I'll keep a joyous heart, I'll dance as I
move, like a flame among flames, I don't need to be incombustible
to walk through fire." These phrases are quite lovely. There are
about ten of them. The last one is most remarkable: "If my distress
beacon doesn't work, I'll open my eyes, I'll open my mouth, I'll
contemplate my situation with joy, I won't move as I wait for your
instructions, I don't need the distress beacon to signal my distress."

In Borschem's mechanical recitations, Wilson keeps sensing
zones of reticence. The Superior shrugs. He sweeps Wilson's doubts
away with a gesture. Borschem isn't feeling anxious, he has been
ready for the dive for years, he's already visited the Bardo a thousand times in his meditation sessions, he knows he can overcome
the perils there.

As one final review before departure, Meyerberh recites some
excerpts from the *Bardo Thödol*, which will be read in its entirety,
without interruption, near the door to the Bardo, so that Borschem

can calculate how many days have passed since he began his dive. Each day corresponds to a precise piece of text. Borschem will only need to recognize an expression, a few magic words, to know where he is in the schedule. Meyerberh recites a phrase, Borschem says its exact location in the book. For example: "The sound will break like rollers on a rocky shore, and you will hear: 'Attack! Destroy! Kill!' while a series of magical syllables fills you with fear. Do not fear. Do not flee." Day seven.

Unfortunately, Meyerberh also mentions parts of the *Bardo Thödol* that Borschem shouldn't have to hear during the experiment, speeches meant to guide the traveler beyond the twenty-fifth day. Borschem identifies them and protests: this part of the book doesn't concern him. He'll be revived at the start of week four. If the monks are reading these lines, it means he wasn't brought back to the land of the living in time.

The instructor assures Borschem that no one's even thought about the experiment failing, improbable as it is. The Bardo doors are in perfect working order, and will be reopened for him on day twenty-five. Borschem really has nothing to fear. Every last detail has been studied in depth.

Borschem doesn't reply, but he appears to be more suspicious than at the start of training. Wilson, for his part, is now certain his brother is going on a suicide mission. He tells the Superior this. Gavianiouk doesn't let him continue, since the departure ceremony has begun.

Several monks have formed a line to the door. They watch Borschem pass by them and whisper magical incantations from the *Bardo Thödol*: "Oh, Compassionate Ones, Borschem is going to leave this world for the hereafter . . . In the Bardo he will have neither friends, nor protectors, nor strengths, nor parents . . . He is entering into silence and darkness, he is going where stability does not exist . . . Soon he will be terrified by the voices of the

Lord of Death . . . Oh, Compassionate Ones, protect defenseless Borschem . . ."

Borschem sits, without breathing, before the iron door, while Meyerberh unlocks the hermetic seals. The metal screeches. Borschem points out that the door opens into a boiler, into something very clearly an oven of some sort, but someone retorts that it is just a corridor. He balks at going inside, but, seeing no other options than entering, he enters.

Wilson, in his turn, accompanies Borschem's departure with prayers: "Oh, Compassionate Ones, save him from the Bardo's long, narrow passage . . . Help him . . . He is powerless. My brother Borschem is completely powerless . . . He comes at the moment when he must go alone . . ."

Sounds of flames, metallic sounds, the door closes.

There is then silence, darkness. We have passed with Borschem into the Bardo. We try to interpret the miniscule echoes and scratchings. We hear Borschem moving. The silence lasts for a long minute. From the other side of what is maybe still the door, we then hear a voice. It is very deformed, as if it has traveled a long time through a pipe. You'd have to be a specialist in order to decipher it.

Borschem listens carefully. He is that specialist. He is dissatisfied with the sound's quality. He complains about the fact that his journey is going to be ruined by poor acoustic conditions. While he is muttering, he suddenly realizes that his clothes are in tatters, and that he has lost his distress beacon. He then understands what the distant voice is reading.

It's a passage found on the last page of the *Bardo Thödol*:

"Oh noble son, if you do not know the art of entering the right seed and do not master the art of entering the right womb, resist the desire to obtain a body and be reborn at all costs. Raise your head, think no more of those who you love who have stayed behind. Even on the last day, you can still avoid returning to the horrible cesspit of life. Take the inner paths, leave all the fetuses before you by the wayside. Enter the large dwellings made of precious metals. Enter the lovely gardens . . ."

Day forty-nine.

This is a passage read forty-nine days after death.

The end of the journey has been reached, and Borschem has not been aware of any of it. He still does not feel the pangs of asphyxia, but he knows they will come soon enough. He didn't notice the seven weeks he spent wandering. As an interloper in the Bardo, he managed to survive, but everything that happened during that time is foreign to him. He has no other perspective. He has no more time to return to the world of the living. The experiment has failed, the tantric team hasn't revived him. Neither will he succeed, apparently, at leaving the Bardo as a fetus. There are no fetuses nearby. There is nothing.

The play ends with a rather distraught monologue by Borschem: "What gardens? What lovely gardens? Everything is dark and silent . . . They've forgotten me. There's no one . . . What am I going to do now? What large dwellings? What inner paths?"

THE COAL COMPANY

The setting's cast is reduced to two actors:
Moreno, underground worker,
Lougovoï, underground worker.

To the voices of the two actors are added the voices of two other characters exterior to the scene:
Kamchatkine, engineer, rescue team coordinator,
Bandzo Grimm, lama.

The scene is plunged in a shadeless darkness. We are in mining tunnel, nine-hundred meters deep. There's been a catastrophe. The two survivors, Moreno and Lougovoï, are unharmed. They have taken refuge in a narrow space, an intact tunnel blocked off by piles of coal and rock. Elsewhere in the mine, the disaster has reached grisly proportions. Flooded galleries, levels on fire, impassable wells, the alcove where Moreno and Lougovoï wait is, in reality, a tomb. No savior will soon come for them.

By intervals, miniscule bits of rubble fall into the dark space. Stones slide and roll over each other. Water seeps from somewhere next to the two men. The sounds are amplified in the encircling darkness.

The two miners have a work lantern with them. They're saving it. They stay in the shadows, not talking much. They cough, they clear their throats. They know their chances of getting out are slim. One of the reasons they refrain from lighting the lamp is that it turns their shadows into horrible monsters. "It's better to stay in the dark," Lougovoï says. "In the light, we look like we're dead. Like two dead men who've just woken up at the bottom of a crypt. It bums me out." The presence of a cadaver nearby also doesn't encourage them to push the shadows away. The deceased's name is Yano Waldenberg; he is three-quarters buried in the rubble. Just his legs are sticking out. To escape this depressing sight, Lougovoï and Moreno leave the lantern unlit.

There are no perceptible human sounds beyond the tons and tons of collapsed material. Despite this, the two miners believe that several rescue teams are already on their way down, descending into the mine to look for survivors. This glimmer of hope keeps them going.

About a meter from where they are sitting, there is a beam to which is attached an emergency phone. The line, obviously, is cut. Nevertheless, Lougovoï keeps picking it up, taking the receiver off the hook, and calling. The operation is a morose one, as Moreno critiques with disillusioned comments. It's improbable that the phone cables could have escaped destruction. Suddenly, there is a dial tone. It's a miracle, contact is reestablished with the surface, and someone answers Lougovoï.

The man speaking to the miners is the rescue coordinator, a vicious engineer, Kamchatkine, who has in the past butted heads with Moreno and Lougovoï over union issues. They have no respect for him, and he, from their point of view, hates them for their anarchism. The conversation with Kamchatkine goes poorly. The engineer describes the magnitude of the damage: the level where the two survivors are interred cannot be cleared for several weeks. His announcement is frank. He doesn't understand how the phone connection is possible and how Lougovoï and Moreno could have escaped death. After a remark from Moreno, the tone escalates. Kamchatkine is only interested in the dead, not survivors, his thoughts concern counting the dead who were part of Moreno and Lougovoï's group, his compassion goes to Yano Waldenberg, an exemplary team leader, duly noted by management, unsuspected of terrorist involvement. The exchanges are so heated that both sides want to hang up. Unable to keep his anger in check, Kamchatkine passes the receiver to Bandzo Grimm, a lama who has come to give support to the disappeared and their families.

His is the presence that makes *The Coal Company* an actual bardic playlet. Bandzo Grimm is a lamaist priest whose spiritual authority is hardly recognized by Lougovoï and Moreno, since neither of them has ever been a fervent practitioner of Buddhism. In their personal history there are plenty of fights with management, affiliations with support networks in armed struggle, but few hours spent in meditation in temples.

Thus Bandzo Grimm's urgent task is to convince the two miners that they will not be ideologically diminished by listening to and following his advice. Lougovoï and Moreno enter into a peaceful dialogue with the lama. Together they talk about death. The two miners have only a fragmentary idea about what is to come after, but the notion that they will walk for forty-nine days before being reborn appeals to them. It's comforting. Bandzo Grimm has a persuasive voice, what he says is calming. After a while, the two men feel an active sympathy for the lama. Time passes, and, to fight against their dreary idleness, they accept Bandzo Grimm's proposition: they will help Yano Waldenberg through his first steps in the Bardo, and, while aiding Waldenberg, they will learn what is essential for leading a good life, along with the fundamentals of good behavior after death. In fact, considering that they are not dying yet and that they are in greater need of psychological assistance than religious, Bandzo Grimm is asking them to prioritize Yano Waldenberg's well-being over their own.

There Lougovoï and Moreno are, tasked with reciting the *Bardo Thödol* to Yano Waldenberg, or rather, in the darkness near Waldenberg's legs, sticking out of the sooty rock. They take turns doing it. Bandzo Grimm tells them the prayers, admonitions, exhortations, and counsels to the dead over the phone, and they repeat them. Sometimes they repeat them directly, without letting go of the receiver, with an evident lack of faith, and sometimes they feel their way over to the dead man, because they have been struck by the power and imagery of one passage or another, and they deliver the lines with gusto. They perform hesitantly at first, as something in their anarchistic convictions urges them to tomfoolery, but they don't sabotage the text. On one hand, the text is beautiful, and on the other, they don't want to disappoint Bandzo Grimm.

Then their feelings change.

They start to despise the solicitude with which Waldenberg must be addressed, all the pomp and circumstance rolled out just to save him. They start to grow jealous of the dead man. Walden-berg gets to walk toward illumination or rebirth, he gets to hear the warnings and explanations every dead person needs to hear so as not to tremble with fear and despair, two voices are at his side taking turns reading the *Bardo Thödol* to him. While they, Moreno and Lougovoï, will die far from the light, alone and afraid, with no one to remind them how stupid it is to fight and struggle to be reborn, only to die once again.

The reading of the *Bardo Thödol* moves into a chaotic phase. Bandzo Grimm continues dictating the sacred text to the miners, but now neither man hardly makes the effort to pass it on in the direction of Waldenberg's corpse. Lougovoï and Moreno sit away from the telephone and remain silent, or they hold monologues or dialogues about Kamchatkine's or Waldenberg's spinelessness, or they ponder their fate, the fates of the privileged, of the proletariat.

They feel even more exhausted.

They cough.

Bandzo Grimm's voice crackles in the dark. It crackles endless-ly. It describes a world of absolute darkness, where every deceased person can easily cross through tremendously thick walls or any other dark obstacle.

Lougovoï and Moreno listen to this in their coal prison, they don't light the lamp, they cough, they clear their throats, and they wait.

MISHMASH AT THE MORGUE

This setting's cast is also limited to two actors:
Becky Glomostro, student,
Verena Lang, unemployed.

To the voices of the two actresses is added the recorded voice of a supplementary character:
Djamling Schruff, lama.

A medical student, Becky Glomostro, has night-watch duty at the Medico-Legal Institute. Her job isn't difficult; it consists primarily of struggling to stay awake. She reads, she makes herself coffee so she won't fall asleep, she watches the motors that keep the housed cadavers cool. For extra pay, she was also asked to take a body out of its drawer at a predetermined time and place a tape recorder near it. The family, it seems, adheres to the belief that a voice should guide the deceased through his first moments in the Bardo. The dead man happens to be a person of note, Hoïgo Iougorovski, who has just been assassinated. The recorded voice belongs to a lama reading the *Bardo Thödol*.

Becky Glomostro wants to break the boredom of her guard. She invites a friend, Verena Lang, to come join her. This young woman has several psychiatric issues. It turns out that she was once sexually abused by Hoïgo Iougorovski, of which Becky Glomostro is ignorant.

Verena Lang's presence disrupts the aseptic calm of the place. Before Hoïgo Iougorovski's cadaver, Verena Lang recounts the rape to which she was subjected, then carries out a trial against the corrupt officials who run the city. She compliments those who fill them with bullets. She starts or stops the tape against better judgment, she switches the cassettes, and she quickly subverts the reading of the *Bardo Thödol*. To get revenge on Hoïgo Iougorovski, she scrambles the instructions spoken to the dead man. She stands in for the lama, sometimes identifying herself so that the dead man recognizes her, sometimes mimicking the lama's voice to give Hoïgo Iougorovski the wrong advice. In order to give rhythm to her words, she uses a lucky gong, a chrome basin meant for disposed autopsy material.

"Unnoble brother," she says, for example, "you who are called Hoïgo Iougorovski, you are now going to meet one of the creatures you tormented with your ignoble member, with your ignoble eyes, with your ignoble riches. You are going to try to escape her, but you won't get anywhere. You'll panickedly run from one side to the other like a beast caught in a trap. She will approach you to make you remember your criminal existence." (Gong.) "Ask her nothing, do not appeal to her compassion. She is not there to help you, but to punish you. You'll try even harder to flee her, and she will stretch ever farther over you to inflict suffering upon you." (Gong.) "In the past the temples told you that you had to become one with the frightening entities of the Bardo to gain deliverance. But they were wrong, Iougorovski. Whether you flee or look for union, your fear will be immense. Listen to me, Iougorovski. Try not to scream, hide the trembling of your flesh. You will try your best to think about something else while she assaults you and defiles your most intimate organs, but you will fail. Your pain and sorrow will be a dead end, you should know that." (Gong.) "I am Djamling Schruff, the lama your family hired to guide you to awakening. Listen to me. You will know neither awakening, nor deliverance, nor rebirth. You are going to be confronted with the ones you crushed beneath all your weight and terrorized with your member, and whom you had the ignominy to look at while you defiled them and while you sprayed them with your sperm." (Gong.) "You will know no rest. They will heap on you terrible reprisals, many and many times over, and, when you try to crawl out of their grasp, they will trap you again and start anew."

Becky Glomostro tries to oppose this sabotage, but, as she holds no esteem for the deceased, she lets herself be dragged into the

cruel ceremony. She in turn addresses Hoïgo Iougorovski with
words meant to mislead him. She is less obsessed with rape imagery than Verena Lang and lets her imagination run free. "Iougorovski," she proclaims, "you are no more, you are in the ground.
You are suffocating, you are struggling. You are a dust-sick bat,
you would like to flit about but you have forgotten how to detach
yourself from the dark ground. Your extremities twitch miserably.
You will never get back up."

To give theatrical weight to their curses, Becky Glomostro imitates Hoïgo Iougorovski's voice. She comically exaggerates his terror, his spinelessness. She gives him grotesque, laughable attitudes.
Hoïgo Iougorovski tries to cajole his persecutrices by offering
them some dollars. He offers to intervene in their favor with the
bloodthirsty divinities. Thanks to him, he claims, they'll live like
queens on the other side.

The situation has some humor, but remains fundamentally violent. The watch night takes on a fantastical tone. Becky Glomostro
and Verena Lang leave reality behind, they enter the world of the
dead and become the infernal instruments Hoïgo Iougorovski
forged for himself by leading a criminal life. The reading of the
Bardo Thödol at the deceased's bedside transforms into a trial, then
an irrational shamanic dance. Toward the end, the lights go out,
the refrigerators stop humming, and it's unclear if the two women
haven't actually fallen into a demonic universe where they must
accompany the dead man or those like him in eternal castigation.

In his direction notes, Bogdan Schlumm insists on the physical
traits of his characters.

"At the start, everything is normal and empty," he says. "There's
nothing troubling about the mortuary's atmosphere. We are in a
world of birds. Becky Glomostro, and then Verena Lang, appear
nude, their bodies covered in feathers. Becky Glomostro has
a pearl-gray face, very pleasant to behold, above which rests an

almost-phosphorescent emerald-green crest. She has amber eyes, still embellished by two downy circles, her hands are dark gray and very clean. Verena Lang is black, shiny, with the perimeter of her eyes dappled with electric blue, and on her stomach and back, gold-brown speckles. Her eyes are yellow, a mad and admirable yellow."

There you have it. If you would like, you may now continue on.

V. PUFFKY

Schlumm entered the cellar like a newborn, head first and chest scrunched, and immediately saw Puffky running toward him. At first, he thought the other man, deprived of visitors for ages, was coming to wish him welcome. In reality, if Puffky was holding out his arms toward Schlumm, it wasn't because he intended to warmly embrace him. He wanted to take advantage of the opening to reintroduce himself into the outside world. He wanted to shove Schlumm aside and get out of there.

"No," said Schlumm. "None of that. Cut it out."

He pushed Puffky back and closed the door after a few blind gropes. The strike plate emitted a voracious screech, then this side returned to silence.

The light was of an inferior quality. Even compared to a weak twilight, it was barely anything. It filtered in from nowhere, it fluttered from nook to nook, and it reluctantly penetrated the eye's depth. Schlumm felt like he was looking at Puffky through a carbon filter. He saw Puffky trying to get around him to the already-closed door, and he shoved him once more. As if he were doing a jiu-jitsu demonstration, he finished with a twist of the fist and a leg sweep.

Puffky fell to the ground, sending up a plume of soot, and snickered. His eyes were remote, and his head—reproduced time and again on interior bulletins within the Organization, accompanied by acrimonious comments on both his character and philosophical vaticinations—had seen better days. Puffky was exhibiting here this half-idiot face and he was snickering. For a moment, the reasons for his glee weren't apparent, but he still fixed his intense gaze on a point behind Schlumm's neck, an intense, malevolent gaze, and Schlumm jumped, suddenly convinced that he was threatened by something hairy. The point was at a spider's height. He turned around quickly.

"What the," he said.

In the space of a second, he had braced himself to smack away a giant tegenaria, or worse. But there was no tarantuloid creature tensed on the black wall or swinging within reach of his skull.

The wall, bare and oily, seemed to be made of blocks of coal. No living thing could have clung to or hung from it. After a moment of fruitless observation, Schlumm forgot the spider hunt and cast his gaze toward the place where an opening had allowed him to pass a few seconds ago. Any handle or lock could no longer be seen. Perhaps that detail, that absence, had been the source of Puffky's troubling jubilation. The door must have been built with a similar material as the walls. It fit into its frame so hermetically that it was like it had melted into the masonry. There was no other discernable solution.

When he had applied to be the one to go down to Puffky, Schlumm had been warned that the mission would be full of anomalies and risks. It would be a nightmare, respites few and far between. Be careful, he'd been told. Always keep your guard up.

Never let it down. He explored the wall with his palm, looking for the vanished door, looking somewhere for a reassuring cleft, and, finding nothing, he returned to Puffky. He had gotten back up and was dusting himself off. He wasn't snickering anymore, though he kept up the psychotic monk's face that Schlumm, by dint of consulting the Organization's press, had ultimately come to enjoy. There was a photo of Puffky beneath each of the articles denouncing Puffky's dissident ravings. This portrait was meant to provoke a feeling of unease and even rejection in the reader, so that from first contact with Puffky, one's judgment would be unfavorable.

From the Organization's point of view, Puffky's ideas were inadmissible. What ideas? Well, for example, the incompleteness of death. Or the ugliness of transmigration. Or the uselessness of prayer during the journey, the ineffectuality of religious knowledge. Or the absolute improbability of an encounter with the Clear Light. And, finally, the infinitesimal odds against anyone being reborn. That kind of blasphemy. Schlumm had skimmed through all that. Not particularly drawn to theoretical research, he had never had any decided opinions on these questions. The polemicists wielded their arguments with an unbearable erudition. Schlumm was mainly interested in images. In illustrations appearing outside the text. Despite his basic mystical education, he understood neither what Puffky said nor what the authorities rebuked him for either saying or not saying. He preferred to examine Puffky's shifty features, his abnormally-distant eyes, his cheeks that had been sculpted by many tics, and, when the photographer had gotten a full-length shot of Puffky, his gnarled hands that nothing would ever ungnarl. To prepare himself for his trip, he examined it all with curiosity for hours.

In the thick penumbra of the cellar, it was difficult to determine whether the photographs had caricatured or fairly represented their model. At that moment, Puffky was brushing his clothes, rags through which snippets of his thin flesh were visible. He was avoiding raising his eyes to meet Schlumm's, and, suddenly, he lunged at Schlumm with a wooden plank.

"I don't belong to the Organization anymore," he shouted. "Beat it, Schlumm! Get out of my way!"

Schlumm hadn't seen Puffky pick up the length of wood, but he worked out the weapon's trajectory. The plank was going to strike him like a saber.

"Oh," he said.

Then, because he had practiced martial arts since he was a child, he sidestepped the attack, neutralized the plank, and, without hesitating, retaliated. He struck Puffky in the solar plexus, but this time with much more force than during their first tussle, when Puffky had tried to escape.

Puffky bounced backward and collapsed, battering the ground with his whole body. He was surrounded by waves of dirt. A cloud of soot rose slowly, reminiscent of a drop of ink spreading in a glass of water. Behind these plumes lay Puffky, in a pitiful state, concealed. It sounded like he was in pain. He hoarsely swallowed air and spit it back out. The soot floated majestically, then fell. It was a silent, black deluge.

Schlumm observed Puffky's incomplete burial. He commiserated with his wheezing. He himself was sunk to his calves in the stuff.

"Listen, Puffky," he said. "It'd be better if we talked things out. I wasn't sent here to beat you up, you know. The Organization only asked me for a report on the results of your research."

"A report," Puffky coughed.

"Yes," said Schlumm.

"My research on what," said Puffky.

For about ten seconds, Schlumm said nothing. He analyzed the shadowy perspectives of the scene that served as a backdrop to this exchange. Near him, the ground was scratched by traces of the brawl that had just taken place and, further away, beyond the asthmatic mass that was Puffky, everything was more or less invisible. Nothing caught the eye's attention. It was too dark. The vertical surfaces had become ungraspable. All that was left was a fuliginous expanse where Puffky had left footprints when, at the very beginning, he had run toward Schlumm. And still, to decipher these marks you had to strain your pupils until they hurt. The marks were soon lost.

"Your research on the black space," said Schlumm. "On the length of the journey preceding rebirth."

"Oh, that's what they're interested in," said Puffky.

"Yes," said Schlumm.

He was encouraged by what he felt was the beginning of a peaceable interaction between him and his interlocutor.

"There you have it," he continued. "The Organization would like to know where you are with regard to your exploration of the world before birth. The world that comes after death."

Puffky sat up on his posterior. Several clods of soot fell off his back and fragmented. Schlumm scrunched his eyelids. Puffky's silhouette wasn't clearly defined. Fat clumps hung down from the edges. Bumps and a few diagonal streaks twisted and turned. A new fit of joviality shook Puffky, or seizures. Or perhaps a series of sour burps. It was impossible to know whether or not Puffky was feeding himself, let alone if he had any digestive problems.

"Nothing new in that area," Puffky claimed once the tremors had stopped. "How long it takes to pass from one world to the next? Nothing new. At any rate, the official sages have already stated the answers."

"Oh, the sages," said Schlumm.

"Them, or their bootlickers," said Puffky. "Their mercenary penpushers who are always drooling over me in their columns. All those ideologues who think themselves researchers. All those *opéra bouffe* lamas."

"There, there," said Schlumm.

"If you want answers, check the *Bardo Thödol*," said Puffky. "It's all in the *Bardo Thödol*. Don't count on me for."

He was interrupted by a coughing fit. He rasped his larynx and expelled a bit of drool into the adjoining shadows. Now he was getting back up. Without shaking off all the lumps sticking to his armholes, he moved his legs and took a step.

He took another step, then several.

Now he was sinking into the dark. He was already shrinking away.

"Hey!" said Schlumm. "Don't leave like that!"

"Leave me alone," Puffky shot back. "Go back to the superficial world, if you think you can."

"Oh, me, superficial," Schlumm protested.

Puffky shrugged. He continued onward.

Seized by apprehension, fearing he'd disappear forever, Schlumm followed him.

The light had faded even more. The ground beneath their feet skidded and packed with a snow-like sound. They were leaning forward and no longer speaking. Thus unfurled ten or fifteen minutes, then a week. From time to time, Schlumm caught up with Puffky and beat him to force him to say where he was going, or to ask whether the cellar had an end or not, or if one of them was dead and which, or if they had both died and how long ago: those kinds of questions. Puffky never unclenched his teeth. He revealed nothing. He kept moving, giving the impression that he knew the way, sometimes going in large loops around a hypothetical obstacle and sometimes taking shortcuts through the dust and pellets, sometimes squatting to rest. He'd taken charge of setting the pace.

The indivisible darkness reigned. In a description of the nothingness that Puffky had once, before his disgrace, been authorized to publish, he'd spoken of a series of moonrises over the black plains, over the colorless powdery dunes, and moonsets over tarry horizons far removed from compass points. But here, no star. There had to be a vault around somewhere, doubtlessly a heavenly one and thus far above them, but no matter what time it was, no star appeared.

When they reached week two, Schlumm started to go mad. The walk had worn him out. He split into several Schlumms, several personalities, none of which were familiar to him. He closed his eyes and tried to look for memories that would have belonged to him alone, so he could give some meaning to his presence by Puffky's side or on his heels. The only thing he could rekindle inside himself was his duty to torment Puffky until the other man expressed himself, and he was fighting with Puffky, but without formulating precise demands anymore. His interest had waned, the reason for the interrogation had been cast out of his consciousness. When he got to conduct yet another round of questioning, he preferred to remain silent, and, from then out, he started holding onto Puffky, keeping his mouth closed. Puffky imitated him. They bashed into each other wordlessly, they continued forward, they squatted to catch their breath, they fought.

One day, Puffky decided to speak.

"The time between death and rebirth is forty-nine days," he suddenly whispered.

"That's long," Schlumm commented.

"Seven whole weeks," said Puffky. "A law of nature. The Tibetans have pronounced it in their books for centuries. Don't tell me you didn't know that."

"Oh, I mean, Tibetans," said Schlumm.

The rancors of childhood had engulfed him without warning. The school suddenly loomed in his memory, with its small windows and rooms through which traveled a glacial wind. He remembered having struggled to learn by heart the seventy-seven secret prefaces to the *Bardo Thödol* and having failed a written examination on the order of the hells during the journey. The teacher's name was Thotori Dordji, like the author of the prefaces', or maybe he was a reincarnation of Thotori Dordji, and, in any case, he would thrash the dunces with whatever happened to be in his hand at the time, religious objects on his desk, silver bells, sacred shells, or other things. While he was being mauled, Schlumm would examine the images of demons painted on the pillars, the walls. Despite the numerous corrections he had received, he remembered no pain. He only felt the shame of having succeeded so poorly at learning the fundamentals of science.

"What about the hell worlds?" Schlumm shouted, as if he were having a convulsion. "In what order do they appear? What about the colored visions? The blinding dull red, the weak red, the blazing vermillion, well? The shining blue? Is it in the same order like the Tibetans said?"

It took Puffky some time to answer. He walked, squatted, exhaled, saying nothing.

Schlumm thumped him on the head.

"Yes or no?" he kept saying.

"During the seven weeks of the journey, you visit several hells," Puffky finally pronounced. "But you never realize this. Nothing looks any different from anything else. It's all an arid parade of blacks."

"I was told there'd be colored visions," said Schlumm.

"You can forget about that," said Puffky. "Anyway, the closer you are to week seven, the less you remember. The less you have the instinct to remember. Even your childhood disappears. Memory shuts down. To fill this void, you can still listen to the voices phonocopied here and there, from outside. But that doesn't do much. You don't even know if it's from the past. You'd like to . . ."

"Do you have any phonocopied voices?" Schlumm cut him off.

"You'd like to love what's been recorded, but you don't recognize anything anymore," Puffky continued, scorning the interruption. "You can no longer translate or claim ownership of it. It's foreign. Hoping for lights overhead is useless."

Puffky sighed violently.

"You feel mummified and listless," he said. "From the thirtieth day onward, you no longer want to keep going."

"You have recordings, grooves on wax?" Schlumm asked again.

"Yes," said Puffky.

"That interests me," said Schlumm.

He pronounced these words with the brutality of a police inspector.

"Because of this illegibility of the self that you once were," Puffky continued, "you stop wanting to explore whatever it might be. Neither the past, nor the present, nor what is to come. This falls over your mind on day thirty-three. It falls over you like a lead veil and weighs you down. That's what I've discovered in my research."

"I'd like to hear these recordings," Schlumm insisted.

Since Puffky was reluctant, he prodded him. They exchanged words and several blows. Puffky fought back, but wasn't on the same level. Though he too had once had a specialized military education, he had never kept his knowledge up to date, and so his boxing was mediocre. He landed five meters away, eyes rolled back, lungs completely deflated.

Schlumm felt no thrill of victory. He was not ignorant of how horrible it was to mistreat those weaker and more intelligent than oneself. Guilt filled his mouth with the taste of charred earth. He quickly tried to mitigate the flavor by diluting it with one or two mumbled sentences.

"I . . . I want those disks," he stammered. "The imprint of those melodies that tell . . . I want to know what voices . . ."

Those kinds of mumblings.

Puffky sat in a meditative pose. Cascades of soot trickled from the top of his chest down to his hips. It came off him like sweat. The heat appeared to have intensified, but, in reality, it was stagnant. As for the silence, it was more impenetrable than during previous fights. Puffky had taken his seat, giving the impression that he would move no further.

Schlumm crossed the distance separating him from Puffky. He bent down, grabbed Puffky by the front of his monastic rags, unless it was by a flap of skin unconnected to his flesh, and shook him.

"I want to hear these phonocopies," he repeated. "I want to hear these phonocopies, you hear me?"

Having completed this sterile show of force, he let go of Puffky. The interrogated man reacted with restraint. He was emitting sweat, tiny sobs, and bursts of laughter. He didn't answer Schlumm.

You could scarcely see farther than the length of your fingers. In all likelihood, the two men were busy coughing in each other's faces. They remained seated, as if in a state of rest. All hatred between them was draining away, the only thing remaining in their interactions a framework of instinctive, irreducible brutality. An obstinate resistance from one to the other.

Innumerable fractions of hours flew by like this, night after night. Week three of the crossing had come to an end. Finally, Puffky swallowed his saliva and, from his lips, let slip new information.

"The phonocopied voices come from the edge of the wombs," he said.

"Oh, so finally you're clarifying things," said Schlumm. "You could have said that before."

"Well," said Puffky.

Schlumm stopped talking for a second, enough time to realize that the information Puffky gave didn't actually clarify things.

"What wombs?" he asked. "You mean the ones from incarnations to come or the ones from . . . The wombs from before, the ones I've already . . . The ones we've already been babies in?"

"You'll see," said Puffky. "Everything is recorded in the jukebox."

"In the . . .?" asked Schlumm.

"The jukebox." Puffky repeated.

"Oh," said Schlumm.

"Behind us," Puffky pointed.

Schlumm turned, then froze.

For a long while he inspected the not-light permeating the space.

"I can't make out a thing," he complained.

"There," Puffky pointed.

"Still nothing," said Schlumm.

He wandered away, groping around in the shadows, the black air. A great mass of soot came off him, it had clung to him during the fights and during the breaks. His hands were shaking. He had some difficulty controlling them, they vainly lost their way before him, but quickly came to rest on a surface. There was a wall made of lukewarm Plexiglas and there was a keypad. A machine was standing there, one that resembled a jukebox, effectively. A fallen-apart jukebox.

"I hope the mechanism still works," Puffky hoped audibly.

"Me too," Schlumm threatened.

"Anyway," said Puffky, "like I told you, don't expect a miracle. The speakers only give out fragments. More than one person's been let down by them."

"What kinds of fragments," Schlumm fretted.

"Lies coming from somewhere else and short liturgical poems in crypt language," Puffky explained glumly. "No actual memories, really."

"But all the same, they're close enough, right?"

"Not really," said Puffky.

"Oh," went Schlumm.

His intonation was lacking in enthusiasm. He was already studying the machine. He flipped a switch. It was a simple toggle button, on which the flesh of his index finger felt an OFF/ON in relief. The jukebox reacted. Its innards glowed stingily, communicating a weak pinkness and some transparencies to certain outer areas. The keypad's frame lit up around its edge. On the perimeter, three purple neon lights attempted a resurrection. The tubes seemed to want to show a sample of what they were once capable of, but the effort exhausted them. The gas, of course, turned purple, but not enough to illuminate farther than the tube's walls. The other lights were dead.

Schlumm tapped the keys. His knowledge of jukeboxes had never been put into practice. He amassed doubts and regrets, suspecting that his inexperience might play tricks on him, but not wanting to lose face in front of Puffky. There was the sound of the current inside the loudspeaker, but no voice, phonocopied or otherwise, chose to reveal itself. For several minutes Schlumm fidgeted above the keypad and waited. The minutes remained infertile.

"You have to put a coin into the slot," Puffky suggested.

"What kind of coin?" Schlumm was dismayed.

"A dollar," said Puffky.

Schlumm frisked himself. The sum seemed enormous to him. His hands could be heard reluctantly rifling or pretending to rifle through his savings or pockets.

"The money-box isn't locked," Puffky stated to console him.

Schlumm was muttering indecisively to himself, but, after fiddling with the fabrics and envelopes covering him for a while, he complied.

"Your dollar is just to trigger the mechanism," Puffky concluded. "Don't worry, Schlumm, you can get it back at the end."

"What end?" said Schlumm. "Listen, Puffky, don't take me for an imbecile. I know for a fact that I just lost my only dollar."

"You had to spend it sooner or later," Puffky remarked.

"Shut up," Schlumm snapped. "It's starting."

In the bowels, several gears had juddered. Galvanized by the dropping of the dollar, the membranes were now transmitting punctured bladder sounds and sweeping sounds. It was hot, stuffy, and dark.

"What if I squatted back down?" Schlumm asked no one in particular.

And, without waiting for an answer, he turned to Puffky.

"It's stuffy down there," he explained.

The jukebox grumbled the start of an inflammatory duet, then stopped and made noises like ruminations. The static contained devastated and almost-human nasals. Little by little, one could wrest from this phonetic paste elements that, in a sense, might claim to have some meaning. This blended with lingering precellar odors, with some kind of molded or trampled memorial clay, with remainders of dreams experienced on the surface world or in the cellar, another time, or elsewhere, and by whom unknown. Those kinds of recent or distant adventures.

There was suddenly an announcement from the loudspeakers.

By Johannes Schlumm, the dynaminister, the machine said. **Sword cast for the bread.**

"Short mass for the dead," Puffky translated.

"Oh," said Schlumm. "It's like that."

"Yes," Puffky confirmed. "They talk in crypt language."

"Are they Tibetans?" Schlumm asked.

"I doubt it," said Puffky. "This isn't their kind of thing."

At that moment, the machine specified that the mass could be performed for any occasion, throughout the entire migration, with immediate benefit for the male or female deceased.

"They're lying," Puffky muttered. "You very quickly lose the ability to listen. There you are, unmoving, deaf to admonitions, when there are any. You've stopped thinking. You float open-mouthed under the soot, as if you were completely detached from your fate. You're not interested in the past or future."

"Nice program," Schlumm commented, then shut up.

Puffky didn't add anything more.

The machine continued palavering. It explained that it was first going to play the *Introit*. Then, there was only a sputtering, a few pulverulences. A blast of air caterwauled inside the pipes and nothing formed from their opening, neither melody nor prate.

"This thing is broken," said Schlumm.

"No," said Puffky. "The silence is part of the *Introit*."

"I still want to speed it up," Schlumm said irritably. "How do you do that?"

"Like you did with me," said Puffky.

Schlumm heavily reared back on his lower membranes, then walked over to the machine and stared at it while clenching his jaws. Then he began kicking it so it would scream out some text. Fluffy curls of dust drifted across the Plexiglas slopes and bounced off, blemishing Schlumm's shoes. The neon lights were not holding up well to the shocks. Their purple sparkled for a moment, then weakened.

While Schlumm was soliloquizing in its company, the machine engaged its modest defense system, spitting out a fetid cloud meant to frighten off possible assailants. The gears, in their distress, eructated into the mucus membranes the miasmas of prisons and medieval dictatorships. If the attacker had had enough energy to reflect, he would have noticed the threat, he would have compared this effluvia to what men and women had inhaled long ago, when day and night they slumbered in hell, in camp barracks or subterranean pits, and maybe he would have moved away. But nothing stirred in Schlumm's memory. He beat the machine for a while with the bruising extremities of his limbs and makeshift weapons, such as his scarf, or fistfuls of compacted soot, or filaments of flesh mixed with a bit of earth or bone.

By now, most of the lamps had given up the ghost. It was getting even darker. Everyone was perspiring. Schlumm's monastic robe, the traditional rags covering his body, could have been wrung like a washcloth. Under the attacks, the machine stood like a humble, substanceless block.

Time passed, then came a moment when Schlumm had already finished his dance. He was no longer moving about or frothing. He was rasping fewer commands that Puffky, though not far away, had trouble hearing.

"Deliver your message," Schlumm was saying. "Talk. I know you can talk."

He was tottering over the demolished keypad.

"Come out with what you're thinking," he was insisting. "Or else, I'll . . ."

Information on the external worlds, the machine decided.

"Oh," Schlumm commented. "It's about time."

Advice for the crossing of observable darknesses, the machine squawked.

"Good," said Schlumm, delighted. "Here we go. It took some time, but here we go."

"You'll see, we won't get far," Puffky warned, then sniffed, like a connoisseur.

"Don't try to influence me," Schlumm said indignantly. "I want to judge for myself, without anyone else."

He returned to his place beside Puffky, his posterior sinking two-thirds of the way into a friable and silky heap, which was like a chair made of friable silk.

Lesson twenty-eight, the machine whined.

"Oh, no luck," Schlumm groused. "Looks like we missed the start of class."

"We'll miss the end too," Puffky prophesized.

"Oh," said Schlumm.

By Bogdan Schlumm, the desperadoboist, the machine continued. **Lesson on deviousness**.

"What the," said Schlumm.

"Shh," intimated Puffky.

. . . Being a vegetable among vegetables. Waiting. Especially that, waiting. Seeing the why of the drizzle or the watering can. Feeling growth, looking for the why of the apple scabs. Not relying on the moon for light. Respecting conformity, not breaking anything, but understanding your roots. Being thus, a rebellious vegetable, dangerous in the humid night. Blocked in every direction slyly cursing. Like in mud sleeping, but not sleeping. Quietly following the movements of the gardener and his spade. Always imagining that you will escape the blade and, at the first opportunity, acting by surprise and swiftly. Suddenly waiting no longer. Suddenly unmuzzling yourself from the earth. Snatching the gardener, splitting him with a violent incantation. Destroying him at the top of your voice. Roaring from your rootlets, splitting and destroying him.

Response by Wolup Schlumm, the dodecaphone.

"What does this gobbledygook mean," Schlumm whispered in Puffky's ear. "I can't catch a thing."

"Shh," said Puffky. "Don't talk at the same time as a dodecaphone."

Seeing a wretched table, a long, wretched table, said the machine. **Hating. Especially that, hating. Heeding the sky-dove's frizzle o'er the slaughtering pan. Pealing croaks, brooking the lie of the dappled crabs . . . Caught me trying all the loon's delights . . .**

"Puns!" Schlumm was outraged. "They're throwing crypt language puns at us!"

Responses and lessons were strung out, impossible to memorize or even follow. The text wasn't a living one, it evoked no recognizable experiences, it presented a complete opacity that disappointed its listeners terribly.

"Wordplay with neither head nor . . ." Schlumm grumbled.

"This is what happens to memory after week three," said Puffky.

"This is worse than death," said Schlumm.

"Oh, worse," said Puffky.

From time to time, the jukebox would lighten the mood by narrating dreamlike sketches taking place in parallel hells to those of the wombs or the surface world. One was thus entitled to supplementary tragicomedy, to the adventures of Abram Schlumm, the egalitarian, or Freek Schlumm, the Untermensch, and even other poets of the same tribe, even more infamous and minor heteronyms. They were expressed in general language, less closed than the dodecaphone's: all the words were intelligible, and the syntax hardly strayed from beaten paths, but, in the end, only a few snippets could be obliquely understood. To make matters worse, between responses and playlets, the machine would sometimes daydream. It muttered exquisite corpses, producing surrealist sayings.

Autopsy believed to take, the machine would say . . . **Out at sea the old garden spider broke the box of clowns . . . We flew away in our own secrets to tell . . . I repeat: we threw away**

**ten-hour foam secrets who yell . . . Without spindrift names,
the bonzesses laughed . . . They had foretold piercing our memories, TOWARD THE PLOP . . . I repeat: they had four gold
piercings of sour mulberries, TO WARD THE FLOP . . .**

While all the responses were being pronounced, an intense non-
sympathy with the texts ran through the listeners' spines. Entire
clusters of nights went by, we remained sitting, growing thinner
in the dark, we couldn't recap anything, repeat anything, we no
longer knew what was happening.

The machine sputtered in its corner, illuminating the surrounding mounds, humps, and clods.

Neither Puffky nor Schlumm stirred or flinched. They were
slumped, side by side, scrutinizing the sole purplish ray to come
out safe from the beating. This smear of color brushed against
their toes so sadly that it incited them to become even more immo-
bile. On account of the scene's drained appearance, and because
of how miserable the light was, it was tempting to imagine the
two men as working a theatrical ceremony with neither plot nor
dialogue, and whose rehearsal had fallen apart. Since the old rags
enveloping them gave them an asexual appearance, they seemed to
be silently brooding on the reasons they had so poorly interpreted
their role as two blind mendicants, perhaps having drunk to forget
their degradation and their fears, now distraught in the disaster's
midst. This brooding was prolonged and inconclusive.

At present, there were few notable differences between Schlumm
and Puffky. Schlumm had aged, his shoes had split apart, his
clothes and even his skin had taken on the indistinctly ragged hue
that without fail betrays the inhabitant of inescapable tunnels,
the guest of what Tibetans, in their fictions, call the intermediary world, claiming, quite wrongly, that it is enough to wander
there for forty-nine days to be reborn in the hereafter or beyond.
Schlumm was now huddling against Puffky, as if Puffky had

always been his best friend. He was no longer holding onto his legs. The heat of the space had defeated him, as well as the appalling idea that there was no womb at the cellar's end, and so no hope of getting out. Whatever the length of eternity might be, he was going to have to get through it with Puffky, without being reborn and without understanding a thing, grasping at echoes he would have to pretend to identify and adopt and love like they came from his own head.

For a brief fortnight, their situation changed little. They meditated and dozed in turns. Their oppressed breathing was palpable. Sometimes, a jolt of somewhat forced joy would shake Puffky, with mad hiccups and shivers. The jukebox was the ultimate consultable archive, the sole spark of intelligence. It grumbled continuously and softly. Everything would have been different if we could have determined whose memories it was adulterating.

Dreamt of you, Schlumm, the machine fleetingly sighed. **Dreamt of you . . . Junks in pocket, you went back up June 27th Avenue, TOWARD THE WOOD STOVE . . .**

"This Schlumm," Schlumm said suddenly. "He reminds me of someone. His face is on the tip of my tongue."

"We're there," said Puffky.

"What," said Schlumm, his voice ponderous, drenched in somnambulism and bister. "What. Where are we."

VI. DADOKIAN

"I am speaking to you once more, oh noble son, oh Schmollowski," a voice says.

A dispassionate voice.

The one speaking is an almost normal tantric monk. A lama like those we have learned to love, by dint of meeting so many of them throughout this story. He is draped in a robe covered in patches, overall raspberry color. Across his chest he is wearing an indigo canvas satchel along with various fabrics of ambiguous significance. His entire being emanates a dusty grandeur. At first glance, his dispassion seems based on much humor, and is not simulated. He tranquilly doesn't give a fig about anything, but he feels no nihilistic anxiety. He could be any age, let's say fifty-one so as not to be accused of lacking verisimilitude, but, to the credulous, he might say, deadpan, that he was born seven- or eight-hundred years ago, or even earlier still, for example before the world revolution. Suppose he tells this to Western adherents who lack common sense.

No objection would arise. This detail, furthermore (his exact age) doesn't concern us.

I said almost normal because he sports an unusual number of talismans, including a discreet lapel pin in the shape of a red star, whose central image has been scratched and wiped away, perhaps out of monastic nostalgia for non-violence or the demands of political prudence, perhaps a sub-machine gun, perhaps a terrorist acronym two or three characters long, perhaps the portrait of a guerrillero or philosopher. The pin is raspberry too. It disappears under a scarf and, from time to time, light falls on it and it gleams.

"Listen to me, Schmollowski," the lama repeats.

He is in the middle of officiating in a Chinese temple, though not in the main hall. At this moment he is standing in the cramped room where the temple watchman naps when the too-heavy heat overwhelms the afternoon, a place serving also as a storeroom for bottles of oil, sticks of incense, two umbrellas, and cartons containing wads of paper money to be burnt for the posthumous comfort of the Chinese dead, so they can purchase essentials in the other world, along with anything frivolous they happen to find on sale. The lama is settled in the middle of this bric-a-brac, after having as always placed a dollar next to the miniscule towel into which the watchman sponges his sweat. Elsewhere, in front of official altars, he would perhaps not be tolerated, as he belongs to a dissident faction, politically and religiously incorrect, often asked to go minister under other roofs, sometimes politely and sometimes with nightsticks. So he visits Chinese districts, choosing places of worship where there is less risk of him being bothered with questions of dogma, but he does not abuse his hosts' hospitality and he steers clear of major idols.

On a carton he has placed a portable gong, one with a clear and short sound, along with a photograph and the heap of hardened pages his personal copy of the *Book of the Dead* has been reduced

to. Facing him, there is a wall blackened with molds and a lunar
calendar surmounted by mythic Chinese generals and ministers
who have absolutely nothing to do with Tibetan tantrism, so they
can be disregarded here. From the ceiling hangs a bare light bulb,
switched off. The only window looks rather like an embrasure, and
is obscured by a pot of flowers. The room is damp, hot, and poorly
lit. Outside noises come in from every angle and crystallize inside:
the comings and goings of the devout with offerings, prices from
the stock exchange in Cantonese that the watchman and temple
seer, both drowsy, listen to with a distracted ear, and, to finish, the
distant sounds of the street: slivers of voices, a motorcycle's vroom
as a handyman repairs it out in the open, horns from buses or taxis
blocked by the crowd. A public market adjoins the temple.

"Listen to me carefully, Schmollowski," says the lama. "I am
Jeremiah Schlumm, a Buddhist lama from the Association of Red
Bonnets Anonymous, a tantric mutual aid organization. The Association has entrusted me with reading to you the *Bardo Thödol* for
forty-nine days. I know you are not a member of the Buddhist
community, but I know on the other hand that you have read and
reread this book, the *Book of the Dead*, during your long stay in captivity. I know you had it in your possession. We sent it to you along
with candies, undergarments, and soap."

The brouhaha of the market superimposes itself on Jeremiah
Schlumm's speech, who has not taken it into account. But suddenly a quarrel breaks out around a medium-ripe durian, which
the vendor is refusing to slice for free. It is a harsh and uncouth
discussion. The lama feels obliged to strike his gong to recapture
the first sound. The merchant sets his price in dollars, the buyer
persists on calculating in the old currency. He demands a discount
since the fruit has not been skinned. The two men are dishonest.
The debate drags on. With a gong blow the Anonymous Red Bonnet dulls the violence.

"Concentrate, Schmollowski," he says. "Even a non-Buddhist can hear my voice. And even you, who have always fought against any and every authority, even you can understand me and can obey my instructions."

Gong.

"It's enough to have skimmed through the book just once to understand me."

Rumbles from the street.

The durian costs a dollar a pound. That's high.

"Twelve days ago," continues the lama, "you exhaled your last breath in cell 2518, which was your home for three decades. Twelve days. If we apply the magical tradition's calculus, that means you have been separated from your body for eight days already."

Gong.

Jeremiah Schlumm readjusts his indigo bag, his scarf. A sunbeam has intruded through the very narrow window. Almost immediately, a cloud intercepts it. The red star-pin glimmers on Jeremiah Schlumm's chest, then fades.

Behind the lama's back, the temple goes through a phase of somewhat slowed activity. The seer opens his eyes, no client is sitting facing him, he goes back to sleep. A devotee is humming a sacred nursery rhyme before a statue of Guan Yin. Out of the blue a coil of incense loses nine centimeters of ash, dissipating between the goddess and an offering of ravioli.

The heat is oppressive.

"Every morning," continues the lama, "I open the file the Association gave to me, and I speak to a photograph of you, the only one the Association possesses, where you can be seen handcuffed, between two policemen. The file contains a succinct biography. It says you spent your youth murdering murderers and destroying the rich's riches, and then you remained at rest, for years without number, between the four walls of cell 2518. Calm and detachment then became your daily life. You lived like a meditant. Sometimes, it's true, your monastic serenity was troubled, especially in the first twenty years, when current political affairs were still hot in the outside world and the guards would push door 2518 open to beat you or subject you to mock executions, or when you heard your male and female comrades beaten, sink into madness, or die."

Gong.

"This time is no more, Schmollowski."

Gong.

"The world of egalitarian struggle, with its prisons and its innumerous defeats, this world is no more, Schmollowski."

Gong.

"For you there is no more world of any sort."

Gong.

The raspberry lapel pin appears once again. Other talismans can also be seen, made to obtain the goodwill of the Five Thunders, or even consecrated to minor heroes of the Great Brood, to obscure gods, to the windy ones. The Anonymous Red Bonnet is emotionless under the bare, lightless light bulb, behind his shield of superstition and divinities. He believes in nothing, he believes in only the void.

"There is only the Bardo in which you are now walking, and the forty-nine days separating your death from your rebirth."

Gong.

"Now, listen to me, Schmollowski, noble son. Don't let yourself get distracted. The first days of the voyage have been lost, since you have not followed my guidance . . ."

Until now, there has been nothing extraordinary about the lama's voice, it fluctuated without static or irregularities, but now something is affecting it, a distortion at first hardly noticeable, then very pronounced, a sizzling distortion, as if it had begun traveling on inorganic supports, as if between Schlumm's mouth and our ears there were now a power cable and very little air, no more air at all, even. In a few seconds, the Anonymous Red Bonnet's powerful words give way to an artificial lowing. The consonants are crushed in an amplifier, the vowels are coming from an echo chamber. The sounds of traffic, the altercations between customers and shopkeepers have been gummed out. A voice can still be heard, a poised and solemn voice, but, it is diffused by a telephonic system much more tantric than technically perfect.

Whether we want to or not, we are no longer in Jeremiah Schlumm's company, with the cartons and bottles of oil, but in Schmollowski's Bardo, and, in a certain way, with Schmollowski, even though he is completely alone. More than one element indicates it. The hermetic darkness, to start, and the silence, as if outside didn't exist. Next, acoustic phenomena that only occur in the posthumous worlds, on account of a certain obsolescence of time and space: for example those sonic effects that scholars have inventoried using the terms mute voice, double arch, residuary mental melody. And finally, the fact that suddenly Schmollowski is speaking and we are hearing him.

For now Schmollowski is well and truly taking the floor. He is soliloquizing.

The unintelligibility and the gong in the loudspeaker recall an announcement in a deserted train station. A station plunged into night, totally dead, with no travelers.

"It's curious, that loudspeaker," Schmollowski mutters. "Every morning for eight days, at breakfast time . . . Propaganda from the R. B. A., Red Bonnets Anonymous . . . Buddhist litanies, unending exhortations . . . A gong . . . E-flat, I think. A splendid note . . . That's a change from waking up to keystrokes on the cell door . . . Much friendlier . . ."

"You have not followed my guidance, Schmollowski," the lama says. "You have not rejoined the sublime Brightness of inexistence.

You have missed the opportunities offered to you and you have continued lamentably to exist in your lamentable self . . ."

"And then," Schmollowski observes, "that monk is nice. He pretends not to be easy-going, but deep down, he's a nice guy."

"Last week," says Jeremiah Schlumm, "the peaceful divinities presented themselves to you one after another. And instead of dissolving into them to become Buddha, you continued roaming the Bardo like a frightened and stupid animal."

Gong.

"Schmollowski! Do you really want to wander like this for forty-nine days?"

"Yes," says Schmollowski.

Gong.

"Schmollowski! Do you really want to roam down there like a dog for forty-nine days?"

"Yes," says Schmollowski. "Even more than forty-nine days, if possible. If I sort things out well enough. Because, so as not to hide anything from you, comrade lama, I like it here." (Gong.) "I like it a lot. I have every intention to stay here, if you want to know. Do you hear me, comrade lama?"

He shouts.

"Do you hear me, comrade lama? I'm going to hang out here! I feel good here!"

His voice floats echolessly in the dark space, then it crumbles.

Just now, when the loudspeaker started crackling, like it did every day now at breakfast time, Schmollowski wasn't surprised. He had been expecting it. His mind wasn't wavering between sleepiness and unconsciousness. His body was resting. He was sitting on the ground, relaxed, his intelligence on the lookout. He soon picked himself up and began walking again, like the day before, like the day before the day before. He's listening to the lama's phrases and soliloquizing as he advances. Right now he is

stamping on gravel, black, friable material. He is stamping on it
with no excessive haste.

"No, evidently, he doesn't hear me," he mutters.

At the same moment, the gong resounds.

"Listen to me, Schmollowski, make an effort to pay attention!"
the monk exhorts. "Remember what you read in the *Bardo Thödol*!
You're facing an astonishing opportunity, seize it! Starting today,
you can end the painful cycle of death and rebirth . . . You just
have to want it . . . Forget what you've lived until now. You always
took it for a journey in the real world, when in fact it was pure
illusion! Disinterest yourself in your past, Schmollowski, your passions from another time! Take advantage of your death, Schmollowski, don't squander it! This journey is a thousand times more
important than the one that preceded it!"

"Yes, yes, I'm aware," says Schmollowski.

He is wearing an anthracite-gray tracksuit with sandals. You
can hear the squeaking of his steps on the gravel and clods of soot,
the sand. Sometimes he slips on the coarse earth, sometimes he
sinks in to his ankles.

"What do you think?" Schmollowski asks. "Sure, I read everything the R. B. A. sent me. Their profession of faith, their explana-
tory brochures, all the material . . ."

Gong.

"I liked it," Schmollowski mutters.

Now that we have grown accustomed to the darkness, we can
describe it with a greater exactitude. A very thick twilight-black
reigns, contradicting every notion of landscape near or far, but all
the same one does not walk through it blindly. Schmollowski, even
if his sandals don't help, is progressing in a straight line without
stumbling, and, after a moment, we perceive that he is following
an already-traced trail. There is no landscape to properly speak of,
no image, but, when we try to imagine the decor, we know that

we are moving through a vast black plain. We trample something that looks like a path surrounded by fields of charcoal. Our eyes don't need to be open for us to realize this.

"Don't worry about me, comrade lama!" Schmollowski shouts at the loudspeaker. "I'm not following your instructions to the letter, but I'm inspired by them. My life in the Bardo is organizing. I'm not squandering it, tell your R. B. A. comrades. I'm fully enjoying my journey, the possibilities offered to me . . . Every morning, at the same hour, I hear your voice announcing the day's program. After that, once the silence comes back, I'm free. Free! My movements, my thoughts, my time. I haven't been this free since . . . oh my! So many years . . ."

"The biographical synthesis at my disposal," says the lama, "assures that you had great qualities, that you were intelligent and sensitive. You put these qualities into the service of social vengeance and egalitarian punishment. They helped you plan attacks, murders . . . You killed quite a lot of people, from the newspaper clippings I see here . . . Camp managers, sellers of misfortune, billionaires . . . But, deep down, you were the opposite of a brute . . ."

Gong.

"You must be able to grasp my words. And anyway, if our priests speak the truth, it's enough to have read the *Bardo Thödol* a single time to remember it completely after your death."

Gong.

Schmollowski acquiesces in silence. The priests speak the truth: the *Book of the Dead* has embedded itself in his memory without a single line missing. He knows it by heart. But, in this precise moment, he is not thinking about the *Book of the Dead*. He is thinking about the material conditions of his stay in the Bardo. They are good, especially if compared to the thousand bothers that spoil the living's lives. The advantages are considerable here. Schmollowski looks them over. No dietary worries. Hunger is unknown. So you don't spend your time looking for or preparing food. You don't eat, you don't digest . . . No digestion, another great advantage. No need to squat in some ditch at any moment to expel foul matter out of yourself. That also implies you don't have to fear stepping in feces. Even if it's where the dead roam like dogs for forty-nine days, you don't have to constantly scan the ground to avoid droppings . . .

"Also," Schmollowski mutters, "physical fatigue doesn't make itself felt, or so little . . . You feel like you're in great shape twenty-four hours a day . . . Otherwise, you'd have to find a place every evening to bivouac, lug around a sleeping bag with you . . . All those idiotic joys of camping. While here, from time to time, I sit on the ground to recuperate a little . . . That's all . . . I sit, I wait for the loudspeaker to signal a new day . . . The comfort is relative, but it's tidy."

Gong.

"Nice and dry, not cold, no cowpies," Schmollowski says.

Gong.

"This week begins a new phase of your crossing," the lama announces.

Gong.

"Wait, a hill," Schmollowski murmurs. "A kind of large sandy pile. I'm going to climb to the summit. See if I can see anything."

"Throughout this second week," says the lama, "you are going to be confronted by irritated divinities, bloodthirsty divinities."

Schmollowski scales the hill. It's a small dune. Despite his declarations on the absence of physical fatigue, the ascent drains him. He arrives at the top breathless and sweaty. He pivots, and, rear first, lets himself fall on the extremely black sand.

"I'm going to take a short breather," he says.

Gong.

"Do not be terrified by them, noble son," says the lama. "They have a hideous appearance, but they are not any less benevolent than last week's divinities. The book we sent you included numerous illustrations, do you remember? You pinned them to the walls of your cell. Recognize them, go and meet them without fear. Renounce immediately everything that made you an individual."

"That's where we diverge, comrade lama and I," Schmollowski mutters.

"Renounce, be one with them, dissolve into them . . ."

"No," says Schmollowski, "*That's* where we . . . 'Noble son, renounce, cease to be a person!' 'Join the collectivity of the nothing!' 'Noble son, cease to be conscious of yourself!' No, there's no way I'd adopt the Red Bonnets Anonymous philosophy. No way I'm accompanying them on this territory. No, really . . . it's too suicidal. I won't walk . . ."

Gong.

"Not for me!" Schmollowski shouts in the direction of the loudspeaker. "Too suicidal!"

"Now at the moment," the lama proclaims, "you are going to be confronted with an enormous, dark-brown being, with three heads, six hands, four legs . . ."

"What haven't they come up with!" says Schmollowski.

There is a smile at his lips. He has always been a connoisseur of post-exotic or fantastical stories and tales, he even composed some of his own in prison. Then he jumps. He stretches toward the darkness while screwing up his eyes, like he's scrutinizing it. His smile fades. Suddenly he's not smiling at all anymore. He's on high alert.

Because now he hears footsteps trampling the night and the gravel, at a certain distance. Let's say some sixty meters away, more or less.

"Hang on," he breathes, "that's right. A form's coming up the trail. It's coming toward me."

"This being will be surrounded with blinding flames," the lama describes, "and it will stare at you while sneering, with its nine large, open eyes, in abominable fixity. Then you will see garlands of skulls and freshly cut human heads swinging across its chest. And, as it approaches, you will notice it walking intertwined with a terrifying goddess. Thus it will progress toward you, while copulating with this irritated goddess, both of them howling and moving about like a nightmare . . ."

"I love it," says Schmollowski. "How I adored that book . . . It's part poetic, part insane . . ."

"Without interrupting her sexual union with the sneering being," continues Schlumm, "the goddess will turn her head around backward to pour the contents of a large, blood-filled shell into her mouth . . ."

It's very dark. Schmollowski however can see enough to make out that the approaching being has only one head.

"Bah, that's not the type to copulate while walking," Schmollowski grumbles. "That's a short, perfectly ordinary man."

Gong.

"Do not fear them, Schmollowski," says the lama. "Neither him, nor her."

"An everyday guy," continues Schmollowski. "He even kind of looks like Müller, the fourth floor guard. The one who strangled Julio Sternhagen with a belt . . ."

"Do not fear them at all," repeats the Anonymous Red Bonnet. "They do not exist. They have no reality. They are no more real than you are. Your mind is what stirs them, your imagination gives them their appearance. Approach them. Recognize them for what they are, which is to say absolutely nothing. Try to vanish into them. Think only on that. Try to be completely absorbed upon contact with them."

Gong.

"If you accomplish this, immediately, you will be liberated."

Gong.

"This guy's looking at his feet as he walks," Schmollowski notes. "He can't see anything."

The man who looks like Müller arrives at the top of the mound, following the length of it without lifting his eyes. He walks without paying attention to anything, zigzagging slightly. He has already started to move away.

"He didn't see me," Schmollowski says.

He stands back up.

"Do not let terror overcome you!" says the monk.

Gong.

"Hey!" Schmollowski yells at the passerby. "Hey down there! Mister! Hey!"

The footsteps freeze. The man is looking for where the voice hailing him came from.

"I'm here at the top of this kind of dune!" Schmollowski shouts. "Come up and take a quick break, it overlooks the plains and is quite nice!"

The newcomer seems to be easily convinced. He hesitates for not even two seconds. Now he's climbing the slope. The crumbly granules roll beneath his feet. He slides backward, he catches back up. He fights against breathlessness, in his turn. Closer up, he doesn't look like Müller. He has on a plaid shirt unbuttoned to the navel, an undershirt and a pair of shorts peppered with oily stains, and tattered sneakers. His appearance is half-pallid, half-crazed.

"Hello," he says. "It's very nice to come across someone. The sky is so black that I couldn't even figure out the height of the sand pile . . . And it's been so long since I started walking all alone. I was certain that other people . . . that there were no other people . . . I mean, do you see what I mean?"

"I'd started to think things like that too," says Schmollowski.

"Have no fear, Schmollowski!" the loudspeaker blares.

"I say," the newcomer chirps, "we've got a damn nice view from up here . . . You can make out the trail for at least twenty meters . . . And it's so calm too . . ."

"Yes," says Schmollowski. "It's a perfect place for calm . . . If only that loudspeaker were gone . . ."

"That what?"

"That loudspeaker."

"You hear a loudspeaker?"

"You don't?"

"I don't hear anything."

"Ah," says Schmollowski.

"You know, if you're hearing something, it might mean you're crazy," the other reasons.

"Ah," says Schmollowski.

"It's not a loudspeaker for me," the other explains. "It's a radio. They implanted a radio set in my brain. In the frontal lobe. It goes off around noon. They read me the day's news, then they go quiet. Back there, at the asylum, they controlled me through the radio. They sent me messages to control me. It worked night and day. Here, they only connect once every twenty-four hours. That's more bearable."

"Wait," Schmollowski says. "I'm not following. Who was controlling you? Where were you?"

"They'd locked me up," says the man. "They'd locked me up with crazy people. Day and night they controlled me. They watched me with invisible machines. In the dormitory, in the hallways, in the bathrooms. They sent me voices. I couldn't escape them."

"A psychiatric hospital?" says Schmollowski.

"Yes," says the other. "With madmen on every floor."

"I was in prison myself," Schmollowski says. "I'd been sentenced to life for political assassinations. My name's Schmollowski."

"Schmollowski?" the other exclaims. "Schmollowski, the banker killer? Gosh! If someone upstairs told me I was going to run into you . . . Have you been slumming around here long?"

"This is my eighth day," Schmollowski says.

The other man emits an admiring whistle.

"Eight days!"

"And yourself?" Schmollowski asks.

"The same. Eight days. Plus the first four, when I stayed by my body, until they took off with it. Until they destroyed it . . . They burnt it, the criminals! They left me to the flames!"

"Well," says Schmollowski. "The body, you know, after a few days, anyhow . . ."

"They left me to the flames!" the other man repeats, in a terribly anguished tone. "They left Dadokian to the flames! What am I going to do, now that my cadaver is no more, huh? What am I doing here, without a Dadokian cadaver?"

"You're Dadokian?" Schmollowski inquires. "Dadokian, the mad banker?"

Dadokian doesn't respond. Panic and tics have deformed his features. He twists his hands, he gesticulates hysterically on top of the dune.

"I can't go back," he cries. "They burnt my cadaver!"

"Calm down, Dadokian," says Schmollowski. "They're going to make you another one in a few weeks."

"How would I know," Dadokian says.

"It's automatic," Schmollowski reassures him. "You just have to walk for forty-nine days and, at the end of the trail, go into a womb."

"A womb," Dadokian grouses. "What kind of womb."

"You'll see, come the moment," says Schmollowski. "There's nothing to do but wait. It'll pass quickly."

Dadokian is restless with nervous shivers. He starts on gestures that don't end and he shudders. From time to time, he hides his head in his hands. It's unknown what is making him panic more, the loss of his cadaver or the prospect of having to slide into a womb after forty-nine days of walking. Sympathetic, Schmollowski wraps an arm around his shoulders and invites him to sit.

Now they are sitting side by side in the black sand. For a moment, they say nothing. They are two particles at the bottom of a black ocean. Two not unfriendly particles. Not unfriendly and even connected by a natural and immediately frank nuanceless camaraderie. In the heart of the shadows, a non-aggressive companion and a friend. Schmollowski comforts Dadokian however he can. He doesn't repeat the bonzes' lessons, himself being neither bonze nor even Buddhist. But he would like to transmit his own way of accepting adversity. He taps him on the clavicle with a communicative tranquility.

"It'll pass quickly, Dadokian," Schmollowski insists.

"No," Dadokian sighs. "We have to wait. And there's nothing more dreadful than waiting. Time transforms. It becomes unbearable. Take, for example, here, this abomination. We're here, on the inside, waiting for death or birth. Can you deal with that?"

"On the inside of what," asks Schmollowski.

"Persistence," Dadokian says in a pathetic tone, "persistence becomes something monstrous, something that . . . For example, Schmollowski. When I was working, before my family and shareholders had stripped me of all my rights . . . Even then, before my incarceration with the lunatics . . . I was aware of the death that would come one day, at a totally unforeseeable date . . . I was obsessed with the idea of this approaching moment whose speed was immeasurable, unknown, I mean it could be very slow or, to the contrary, as fast as lightning . . . I didn't think about anything but that . . . You know, Schmollowski, I actually wasn't a very morbid person, I . . . I hated death, the prospect of it made me physically sick . . . Do you find that normal, having to live while waiting for death? With a definitive interruption in your future and nothing else? In any case, I was forced to forget that that was going to befall me . . . Dang, unless you're a village idiot or an immortal, how can you just forget that? They wanted me to ignore something that makes all action meaningless, all logic meaning-less, makes existence hellish and meaningless . . . I tried to put on a happy face, but in reality I waited for death day and night, it was frightening because it could come at any instant, but also because it didn't come . . . The wait crushed me . . . One day more . . . And one day more . . . Persistence became excruciatingly heavy . . . Do you understand, Schmollowski? Persistence exists just to hurt me . . . It's lost its meaning . . ."

Pressed against Schmollowski, Dadokian lets his heart out in torrents. Sometimes he sobs or moans. His speech is a jumble of confused syllables. They must be translated to get to their heart. Also sometimes Dadokian becomes quiet, petrified by disarray or shaken with tics. Schmollowski remains quiet as well. With his arm around Dadokian's shoulders, he imagines himself as an Anonymous Red Bonnet receiving the fears and pain of another human, another victim of the terrible human condition. He looks at the black tracks at the bottom of the black dune, he thinks on the horror of life and of death, he listens to Dadokian and consoles him.

"One day," Dadokian continues, "they started sending me mes-sages . . . They tried to control me with short waves sent directly into my skull . . . While sleeping or not . . . And it got worse and worse . . . Even more than death, I began waiting for those messages . . . I knew they would speak, but I didn't know at what moment . . . Do you see what I mean, Schmollowski? It's like we're stuck, we wait for it, it comes or it doesn't come . . . We're afraid of waiting, we're afraid of no longer waiting . . . Time shortens or lengthens forever . . . It's like torture . . ."

"I know that feeling, Dadokian," Schmollowski says. "That's what you feel in prison while serving a life sentence. You can't stand the idea of life or the idea of death anymore. Time's flow becomes unbearable . . . It's a torture, yes."

They ruminate for an hour or two. They are sitting, thinking about the ordeals they suffered while alive. It comes to Schmollowski to turn toward Dadokian. He is still shuddering in his plaid shirt whose color is indefinable, in the shadows. Tics pull at the top of his right cheek. Schmollowski puts a hand on his forearm. Dadokian stifles a whimper.

"What kinds of messages?" Schmollowski asks.

"They sent me absurd messages, to mock me, or messages on the progress or delay of my death. On some days, they informed me that everyone was in the same boat, balanced between the dreadful and the useless, obligated to pretend not to care. The poor and the rich alike . . . You know, Schmollowski, at the time, I was one of the rich . . . One of those you took down with a rifle . . . Eh? You took them down, eh?"

"Yes. In the past."

"With a rifle, yeah, Schmollowski?"

"Yes, with a rifle, or a pistol, when they were close up."

"Alright," Dadokian says.

They sigh a little. They are recalling images from their distant pasts.

"There you go," Dadokian picks up. "So I decided to reduce that universal suffering . . . Since I could, yeah? I thought it'd be good to divide the world's wealth into equal parts between everyone on the planet . . . Starting with the bank I directed . . . Was I wrong, Schmollowski? Huh? Tell me, you specialized in bankers. Was I wrong?"

"You were right, Dadokian. I was already behind bars when you . . . It made noise. Even in the high-security sector, information circulated. I remember. It was in . . . I don't remember the year. A banker applying our minimum program! It was beautiful, Dadokian! It was beautiful!"

"Afterward, they put me in a madhouse. I was in the incurables wing. Does incurable mean anything to you, Schmollowski?"

"No. I was in with the politicals."

"Ah, that's right, yes. So they put me in there. The stockholders settled the problem in no time at all. My children too. The bank wasn't divided into six-billion parts, in the end. They took everything away from me. My only possessions were my cadaver and my toothbrush."

Dadokian goes quiet. He is quiet for another hour, then he starts again:

"We are all prisoners within our flesh and within walls. But those on the outside, why are they waiting to go mad? The parading princes, those who can buy everything with their dollars, one can understand how they resist. Strictly speaking. But the others? Huh, Schmollowski? The others?"

For a minute, Dadokian loses himself in insane mutterings. Suddenly, he returns to his normal elocution.

"Oh! Excuse me, Schmollowski," he says. "I have to cut myself off here. My radio's started back up again. Do you hear it?"

"No," says Schmollowski. "For me, it's a loudspeaker. It doesn't broadcast anything during the day. Besides at daybreak, I just have silence."

Dadokian shivers, as if a spider was running across his face and bothering him.

"Got it," he says. "They're sending messages right into my head . . . Can you hear them now?"

"No," says Schmollowski. "They don't go from head to head."

"Do you want me to repeat what they're telling me?" Dadokian proposes.

"If you'd like," says Schmollowski.

"Oh noble son, Dadokian!" Dadokian proclaims in a solemn voice. "Do not fear that which is facing you, dark green in color, and which in its numerous hands shakes sometimes a club, sometimes a bell, sometimes a scalp dripping with large drops! It's only a bloodthirsty divinity, the divinity of the fourteenth day!"

"The divinity of the fourteenth day . . ." Schmollowski whistles.

He whistles through his teeth. He is dumbstruck. Fourteen. That doesn't match up with the number of days he thought had passed in the Bardo. That's a lot more.

"That's what they yell into my ears from inside my skull," Dadokian says. "Crazy threats. They don't leave me alone . . . They control me . . ."

"We're already on day fourteen," announces Schmollowski. "You see, Dadokian, it's going by quickly, and we don't even notice."

"Even after my rebirth," Dadokian laments, "even when they've forced me to inhabit a new body, they'll continue to control me . . . to talk to me inside my head . . . You can't escape their short waves. They have imperceptible systems . . . They'll find everyone . . . Even if I hide in a new body, they'll find me . . ."

"Calm down, Dadokian," Schmollowski says. "Don't be scared."

"And then, once they've reincarnated me, I'll have to wait for death all over again . . . That torture will start anew . . ."

"We're not there yet," Schmollowski reassures him.

"And then, hang on, right now," Dadokian whines. "This horrible wait they're imposing on us . . . The walk to the wombs . . . Waiting to be reincarnated, waiting for life . . . Waiting for them to give us a cadaver, as a parting gift . . . What if they make a mistake? What if they put me in a bad fetus, huh? If I end up in the body of a spider, for example? I hate spiders . . ."

"Don't throw yourself into your fears, Dadokian," says Schmollowski.

"Listen, Schmollowski," Dadokian panics. "What if they shove me inside a spider?"

Dadokian trembles. He's risen, he takes three steps one way, three steps another. He passes by the mound's edge, where the slope starts, and he goes back. Schmollowski doesn't accompany him in his panic. To the contrary, he finds him, he pulls him by his shirt's sleeve, he embraces him somewhat, making him stay in place.

"Calm yourself, noble brother," he says.

He has taken on the intonation of a Red Bonnet. He has chosen to exercise on Dadokian the peaceful authority of a bonze. It is not out of a taste for deception, but because he hopes it will better combat Dadokian's suffering.

"Find your serenity," he says. "Nothing around you is frightening. Do not fear what is happening to you."

Dadokian is shaken with spasms, but he soon stops moving so disorderedly. Schmollowski speaks to him for a minute more as if he were a monk, then he lets an amicable silence settle between them, then he returns to his normal voice.

"We're going to get out of here," he promises. "We're going to get out, both of us."

"Schmollowski," says Dadokian, "you won't let me fall, will you? If I'm reborn as a spider . . . or even a banker . . . You'll squish me right away, right?"

He's having trouble catching his breath.

Schmollowski doesn't respond.

Everything around them is black, there is no change in the sky no matter the hour. The trail at the bottom of the dune can be seen, but, after several meters, the footprints dissolve into the shadows.

After Dadokian's crisis, Schmollowski sits back down on the ground. For a moment, he thought about leaving the dune's summit and disappearing, but he reconsidered. He could have said farewell to Dadokian and left his side, to follow his destiny, but ultimately, he stayed. He knew Dadokian needed him, which figures into his consideration. Let's not forget that Schmollowski's actions are guided by a solid egalitarian morality, to which is added some elementary Buddhism. He's folded his long skinny legs back underneath him and is meditating. Dadokian imitates him. Now and then Dadokian gives in to a few sobs, a few grouchy sniffles, but, for the most part, he is plunged into a sort of meditation as well.

The silence goes on, then Schmollowski breaks it.

"Here's what I think," he says. "We could try to sabotage this womb business."

"Mmm," says Dadokian.

"Since I arrived here I've been pondering that," Schmollowski says. "It's unbearable, really, to have to be reborn. To have to reintroduce yourself to the world of prisons, asylums, rich people, and spiders."

"Oh, you see?" Dadokian warms up immediately. "You think like I do too, eh, Schmollowski?"

"But how to avoid reincarnation?" Schmollowski continues.

"Yes, hmm. How?" Dadokian ponders.

"The *Book* offers one single method. It suggests annihilating yourself in the Clear Light. And I don't like that."

"Me neither," Dadokian declares indignantly. "Annihilate yourself! They've thought of everything to destroy us completely!"

"I've been thinking of something else myself," says Schmollowski. "We'd need to try to build an inhabitable world here. Understand, Dadokian? We'd need to succeed at sustaining ourselves indefinitely in the Bardo."

"Here? On this sandheap?"

"Here, or elsewhere, a little farther away. We could build a nice refuge, a landscape . . . I've studied the *Book* well. We're in neither space, nor time. Most of the images come from our imagination. If we found a way to stabilize them, materialize them around us, we could reorganize the Bardo to our liking . . ."

Dadokian directs his crazed physiognomy toward Schmollowski. His gaze is no more demented than that of an ordinary madman. He aims it at Schmollowski with hope.

"We'll have to hold on tight when they try to force us into a womb," Schmollowski continues. "On the forty-ninth day, we won't be able to rest at all. We'll have to train ourselves to resist. But after that, Dadokian, after, we'll be able to relax. My loudspeakers will shut off. Your radio will go quiet."

Dadokian fidgets.

"Well now, Schmollowski," he says, "I like that idea! I really like it! You mean we'd stay here outside of time . . . Without any prospect of reincarnation, or death, or . . ."

"We have to give it a shot," says Schmollowski.

"Oh, I like it!" Dadokian exults. "And we'd create the world around us ourselves?"

"That's the principal," Schmollowski confirms. "But wait, there's a condition: we'll first have to succeed at overstaying our welcome in the Bardo past day forty-nine. Fight against getting sucked up."

"We could invent a landscape . . ." Dadokian daydreams. "A pretty little historyless corner . . . No sulfazine injections, no head nurses . . ."

"No nightly beatings," Schmollowski finishes off.

Both of them are absorbed in their delightful reveries. Tics electrify Dadokian's pale cheeks.

"For example," Dadokian says suddenly, "I've always loved the ocean, the waves breaking on the shore, the fizzing foam that appears when the water draws back . . . Say, Schmollowski, couldn't we invent ourselves a little seaside resort? With palm trees, some sky . . . Laughing bathing beauties . . . And we'd be sitting on the sandheap, yeah? Without the torture of waiting . . . Time wouldn't pass, we wouldn't have anything to wait for, never, not even mealtime, yeah?"

"Actually, I don't know if we'll be able to make a paradise," Schmollowski abruptly begins to doubt. "It depends on . . . I don't know what or who it depends on . . . On you, maybe, Dadokian, or me, or even our common capacity for . . ."

Gong.

"Did you hear that?"

"No," says Dadokian.

The gong rings once again. The note is beautiful. An E-flat fourth.

"It's the loudspeaker," Schmollowski says. "The Red Bonnet comrade's about to speak. He hasn't expressed his opinions for quite a while."

"I am addressing you as I have every morning since your death, Schmollowski," says the lama. "Listen to me, Schmollowski!"

"Do you hear it, now?" asks Schmollowski.

"Nothing at all," says Dadokian.

"Oh," says Schmollowski.

Gong.

"I am addressing you for the fortieth time, Schmollowski! Very soon you will no longer hear my voice!"

Gong.

"You are now in the final week of your ordeal in the Bardo, noble son. The wombs are extremely close!"

Gong.

"And in the evening, if there is an evening," Dadokian specu-
lates, "we'll freely return to the asylum, or prison, yeah? We'll still
need a roof, in case of scattered showers . . ."

Schmollowski has stood back up.

"The seventh week," he rasps. "Time's been passing by at top
speed while we've been chatting! Did you know that, Dadokian?"

"What?" Dadokian says, finally alarmed.

"It is high time that I explain to you how to choose the right
door and not be reborn into a form even more miserable than that
of a human being," says the lama.

"What's happening?" asks Dadokian.

"It's all over," says Schmollowski. "The sea resort, the beach,
the laughing beauties . . . It's all over, Dadokian! We've already
reached day forty! We're not prepared! The wombs are close!"

"But . . ." Dadokian stutters.

"We're going to be reborn!" Schmollowski exclaims.

They are there, standing, despondent, for a long moment. Let's
say an hour or a little more. Let's say a day. They appear petrified.
Even Dadokian hardly fidgets. Two miserable men, fixed on the
summit of a sandheap, numbed by bad news, unable to react.

Then Schmollowski comes to life.

Wordlessly he steps onto the slope. His ankles disappear noisily into the dust. He isn't concerned about balance. Sprains don't
worry him. He wants to go fast. He trots toward the bottom. Several seconds later, he is at the foot of the mound. Straight away he
can be heard kneading the gravel with his fists.

"Hey," Dadokian asks, "what are you doing?"

"Quick," says Schmollowski. "We still have a small chance to
stay here!"

"What," Dadokian stammers.

He is still slumped at the top of the mound.

"We have to dig," says Schmollowski. "That's the only thing I can think of. We have to bury ourselves before the wombs grab us!"

He attacks the hill of black sand. He foresees a cavity just at the base, a hole he can bury himself in. He foresees packing himself inside in a folded position, like a bat in hibernation or a Nazca mummy, and triggering an avalanche at the last moment that will bury him, on the last hour of the forty-ninth day. Now, to stay here beyond the fateful day, he sees no other option.

He digs. Matter slides over his arms, flows. Without any shovel to get rid of the gravel, without any plank to fortify the walls, it is very difficult to construct a suitably-sized cavity.

Dadokian has left the viewpoint, in his turn. He stalks around Schmollowski with despairing gestures and jolts. He leans on the edge of the funnel Schmollowski is trying to enlarge, and where enormous quantities of black matter ceaselessly flow back into.

"Move, Dadokian!" Schmollowski snaps at him. "The forces of reincarnation are going to be unleashed, this isn't the time to slouch!"

"I'm receiving a radio message," announces Dadokian. "There're only three days left."

"It's approaching," Schmollowski pants, "it's coming fast! Go on, dig yourself a shelter, Dadokian! Or you're going to be sucked up by a womb! By a spider womb, or something even worse!"

"Where am I digging?" Dadokian asks, distraught.

"Anywhere," says Schmollowski. "There, yes. A little farther even. So your gravel doesn't fall into my hole."

Dadokian rushes on all fours. Feverishly and without any competence in earth working he thrashes about. He has adopted the technique of a dog burying a bone. With his hands he scratches and expels the black granules behind him, between his legs. Following Schmollowski's example, he works at the bottom of the hill. The matter doesn't resist under his fingers, but it is completely uncontrollable. As soon as he makes a small trench, it collapses into itself and fills back in. With anguish he starts his dig over.

"I'm not getting anywhere," he whines.

"Continue, noble son!" Schmollowski shouts. "Your fate is in your hands! Don't lose courage!"

The two men hurry, never stopping. From time to time they speak to each other. They hail each other with anguish and friendship. Depending on the sentence they speak formally or informally. The imminence of the end weighs them down, but each one clings to the other's presence so as not to lose reason, and dialogue between them still exists. They continue exchanging information about what is happening. They break off their amateur grave digging work for four seconds to talk.

"According to the radio, everything will be over in two days!" Dadokian gesticulates.

"Don't stop digging, Dadokian!" Schmollowski yells. "Make your hole bigger! The sucking starts soon!"

They no longer see each other, but they can still communicate vocally. I think there is no more light. In any case, they don't open their eyes, because of the dust. Something has begun blowing dreadfully, an inhaling wind.

"It's blowing dreadfully!" Dadokian says, terrified.

"Bury yourself, Dadokian!" Schmollowski screams. "Bury yourself, noble son! Enter no womb! Do as I do, sink into the gravel! Refuse rebirth!"

"They're still sending me messages!" Dadokian moans. "They're teaching me how to close the wombs' doors! I don't understand anything they're saying! Just one day! It's the last day! I don't have time to learn!"

"Sink into the ground, Dadokian!" yells Schmollowski. "Don't listen to their advice! Hide, open nothing, close nothing!"

Schmollowski's voice is suddenly cut off, as if it had never existed.

The wind continues to blow in the reverse direction of wind, then it calms.

No one knows what's become of Schmollowski.

The space is black.

Dadokian is speaking again. He had perhaps an additional delay, compared to Schmollowski. Let's say maybe a quarter hour more.

There, now his voice can be heard. He is monologuing.

"There's no more gravel around us," he says. "Only a spidery smell . . . Schmollowski! Do you smell that? Where did you go?"

Schmollowski doesn't answer. Dadokian is alone. He is alone, he salivates from fear onto his dirty shirt-front, and suddenly reality appears to him. Whether he wants it or not, life is once again going to take hold of him. Incapable of staying on his legs, he curls up. He has no more strength.

"Schmollowski!" he stammers. "I see spiders mating . . . webs moving . . . They're going to make me be reborn in here . . . Schmollowski! Help me! I've gotten tiny, they've folded me up in here, I can't move anymore . . . Schmollowski!"

Gong.

"Schmollowski!" Dadokian yells. "Squish me!"

The gong vibrates. It's a moon in reduced dimensions, made of a dented and dark metal. The moon vibrates.

"Now my reading comes to an end," says the lama.

And he strikes the center of the moon with an ebony mallet.

"Seven whole weeks have gone by since your death," says the lama. "Today I think of you with nostalgia, Schmollowski, for we will no longer have the chance to be in contact. I will no longer address you, I will no longer speak to this photograph and these policemen."

Gong.

"I will miss it. You were likeable, noble son."

From the other side of the walls, the market's rumble rolls incessantly, with ebbs and flows and moments of sudden swelling. Voices mix with the thousand rustlings of vegetables, fruits, dollar bills. It's going to rain, the afternoon is so gloomy that the lama has lit the room's lamp.

"I do not know how your stay in the Bardo went," says Jeremiah Schlumm. "I hope my advice was useful for you. My powers are limited, I am not even certain you heard me, I am unable to guess what happened to you during your wandering through the Bardo."

"Schmollowski!" calls Dadokian's very faraway voice.

Gong.

"I do not know if your stay there did you good or not," says the lama. "I have no way of knowing."

He contemplates Schmollowski's photograph, then puts it away in the folder provided by the Red Bonnets Anonymous. Later, he will throw it into the brazier that smokes almost constantly inside the temple.

"What had to be carried out has been carried out," he says.

He leans against a crate of cardboard gold bars. Molds contaminate the wall. In the watchman's storeroom, it is very hot, hotter than on the first day of his reading. Jeremiah Schlumm wipes his forehead. His scarf moves, unveiling the red star pin, with its faded machine gun.

"Today," says the lama, "you are either liberated, or on Earth once more, in the form of an animal or human fetus. I wish you the best, Schmollowski. I hope that everything went well for you. I hope that you are no more."

Gong.

Noises from the street.

"From the bottom of my heart, I hope that you are no more," repeats the lama.

He strikes the gong one last time, then he gathers his belongings and goes.

Now, he has turned off the ugly lamp swinging above his head. Darkness has invaded every recess.

"Schmollowski!" Dadokian screams again. "I beg of you, squish me!"

VII. AT THE BARDO BAR

At night, when cars speed down the boulevard, their breath rattles the bar's windows. During the day, as conversations and comings and goings permeate the room with a permanent murmur, the trembling glass jingling in its frame goes unnoticed. But at night, it's a different story. Everything is much calmer after sundown. Consumers disappear, traffic becomes scarce. A heavy vehicle passes by, rumbling, the windows vibrate, then nocturnal silence is reestablished. The neighborhood is deserted. It can be found at a little-frequented exit from the city, far from residential buildings, just next to the zoo. It's clean, there are trees, long black railings, animal growls, but it's deserted. The only inhabited building in the area, with the exception of the drinking establishment, is a Buddhist place. Buddhist or rather lamaist, if one holds to the nuances of pointless denominations, adjoining the bar. An old garage transformed into a temple. Recently transformed into a temple by a semi-dissident association of Red Bonnets. These new religious activities have not attracted any more night owls to the bar. From time to time a devotee will come in, inhale a cup of fermented milk with a straw, and then go. That is the total clientele growth. To summarize, hardly anyone is seen here in the dark hours, when the zoo's doors are closed.

A truck approaches and roars in front of the bar. The windows clatter. Once again, silence sets in.

Behind the counter, the bartender wipes saucers, glasses, cups, teaspoons, puts them away.

Festoons of multicolored garland can be seen outside, suspended there like on a sixties pizzeria façade. Inside the room, the lights are mundane and bright. An hour earlier, there was ambient music, indistinguishable rock songs like those heard in any public place for the last two centuries, but the bartender had turned the volume down when he began his shift and looked for a more exotic station. He came across a Korean music broadcast. It seems to be a cassette alternating between pansori excerpts and traditional dances playing on continuous loop. Sometimes the music is substituted with a Korean commentator who chatters at length in her language, with seductive tones that make Yasar the bartender daydream.

All is calm. The silence is also intruded on by noises originating in the neighboring lamaic temple. Monotonous chants, rhythms lacking any diversity, a prior's solemn voice, bells: on the other side of the partition, a ceremony has begun.

"Could I get another caffeine, Yasar?"

Freek is sitting on a stool at the bar. He is the sole client. It is apparent at a glance that he is lacking something human. For an Untermensch, he is very handsome, but his body emanates an impression of anomaly. An indefinable touch of abnormality pushes him back into the outskirts where the human subconscious hates to venture. He knows this, he tries hard not to let it bother him, but he suffers from it. It doesn't make his relations with others any easier. When he speaks, his voice is often filled with emotion, like with all hypersensitive individuals. It is emotional and slightly weird, as well.

The bartender halts his wiping. He thumps the percolator's coffee filter on a drawer, he screws it back on, clutching it tightly, he slides the drawer back without closing it, he presses the hot water button. His movements are calm. His entire person inspires trust.

"This is your fourth cup, Freek," he says. "It's going to make you sick."

"Don't need to sleep," Freek explains. "Have to go back to the zoo. The animals are waiting for me. Have to talk to them. They're anxious, they're not sleeping. They're afraid of dying."

"Ah," says Yasar.

"I have to reassure them," Freek continues after a silence. "They've smelled death's odor. They're afraid of dying like the clown, like the yak."

Yasar has turned back around. Now, he is placing a bowl of piping hot caffeine in front of Freek. Freek thanks him.

"What clown?" Yasar asks. "A clown died at the zoo? Tell me about it, Freek."

"No, the yak is the one who's dying. I need to go to the zoo because of him. The yak is old and sick. The veterinarian came, he said he still had a day or two. This is the yak's final night. It's happening, in a zoo. The bars protect, but they don't stop death."

Freek pauses. Facing Yasar, who is friendly with him, he doesn't have too many problems expressing himself. It's even the opposite: he seems unable to keep himself from speaking. He dunks his lips in the too-hot caffeine, then revives his talking points.

"The animals are sad behind the gates," he says. "And sadness is very tiring. They're in a safe place, they're protected, but they grow old just as fast as if they were free, exposed to danger. The yak's gotten old. He's been feeling very unwell. The nearby animals are worried, they can smell death's odor. The veterinarian arrives.

He says that the yak only has a day or two left. He says this in front of the yak as if the yak were deaf. He takes out a syringe, he injects useless vaccines against old age and death. Then he leaves. It's night. The smells spread. In their cages, the animals breathe in the smells. It scares them. I have to go and console them. None of the animals can sleep in the zoo at night. They need someone by their side. My words reassure them. The yak needs someone by his side too, to talk to him and help him get through the night. I need to talk to the yak if he's struggling against death, or even if he's already stopped breathing."

In the neighboring room, a bell rings, a very solemn voice pronounces syllables incomprehensible to those who have not mastered Liturgical Tibetan. Then it stops and, coming from a transistor located behind the bartender, there is a Korean melody. It's a tune sung when worn out, when fate has been unfavorable and it's hard to find the necessary energy to go on. A woman adjusts her despair with the violence specific to pansori singers, a violence devoid of any whining, then the chorus picks back up and gives it a more lively coloration, as if the intervention of the collectivity had diverted the sorrow toward new reasons to fight together and endure.

"Excuse me, Freek," the bartender says. "I'll get back to this in a bit. You said something about a clown."

"Yes," says Freek. "Furthermore, that's what's got the animals frightened horribly. After closing time, the clown was found in the raptor exhibit. The clown's cadaver. That's keeping them from sleeping too. The clown's remains in the cage. Smells are stronger in the dark. The animals breathe them in. All the animals in the zoo. They grow restless, they're afraid. They turn in circles or shrink into corners. They think about the yak, about death, about old age. They think about the clown. I have to go back to the zoo to calm them down. So they'll be taken by sleep and forget."

Yasar leans on his elbows in front of Freek. He's just thrown out
the rag he was wiping dishes with. He has the hard face of a man
who has suffered, cheeks scarred from smallpox, piercing eyes. The
beginning of a tattoo can be seen at the base of his neck, perhaps
a souvenir from some journey or passion, perhaps a souvenir from
prison. He's spent a large part of his life within four walls, in fact.

"I still don't understand this clown thing, Freek," he says. "I'm
trying to picture your words in my head, but some of the details
escape me."

"Oh," says Freek.

"Yes," says Yasar. "It's all clear for you, because you're going in
and out of the zoo all the time, like you were . . . as if you belonged
to a world that . . ." (He sighs.) "But I'm having trouble putting the
clown in the scene. I can't figure out what he's doing in the cages
in the middle of the night. You'll have to explain it to me."

"The clown worked in a circus. The Schmühl. Do you know
about it?"

"No."

"He killed himself," Freek says. "He was brought to the zoo
an hour after the gates were closed. After the visitors, children,
left. They do that. A lamaist mutual aid group. You have to sign
up. The clown was a member, I guess. It's a special service. They
get permission from the city council. There are rules. They follow them. They only go into the cages if the zoo director gives
them the green light. They come with the body. There are three
of them. Dressed like gravediggers with nothing to lose. Poor guys
like us, you know?"

"Not really."

"Like us. Wearing civvies. They go into the aviary with the
body. Sky burials, they call it. Sky burials."

"They give the body to the birds to eat?" Yasar asks.

"Oh, not all of it," Freek clarifies. "Otherwise they'd have to wait for days around vultures, eagles, condors. They don't stay long. The zoo's watchmen say that it's mainly symbolic. Some strips, some small slices. A pittance. The raptors are afraid, they don't approach. They won't eat any meat under any circumstance. Afterward, the guys walk out with the body. They load it on a little cart and cover it with an oilskin canvas. No one is on the paths. Zoo administration doesn't attend these things. The zoo is empty. It's already dark. They leave with the body to go incinerate it. They leave, but the dead clown's scent continues to waft from cage to cage. It's powerful in the large aviary, but not just there. It hangs around the zoo for hours. It gives everyone the heebie-jeebies. If no one comes to speak to them, the animals will tremble with fear all night . . ."

There is a silence. The music is followed by applause, then the Korean commentator launches into a dense monologue, without pausing, in which neither Yasar nor Freek is interested.

"Sky burials . . ." Yasar says thoughtfully. "A very, very ancient custom, it must go back to prehistoric times. I've heard about it, but I didn't know it was still practiced. I'd have never guessed that it could happen here, in the middle of the city. Today. Just a kilometer from here."

"There are rules," says Freek. "You have to be patronized by the group, the lamas have to give their permission. And you especially need authorization from city council and written consent from the zoo director. But the vultures aren't asked for their opinion. The vultures don't really cooperate. They're afraid of people who come into the aviary and throw clown meat at them. They don't like to eat circus artists. I'll have to speak calming words to the vultures too. I'll go to the aviary later."

"This clown, do you know any more about him?" Yasar asks.

"He killed himself," says Freek. "There were two of them on the bill, always together. Blumschi and Grümscher. Blumschi and Grümscher, the kings of laughter. One small and one big. I went to see them in their circus, last month. It's losing speed, a poor circus with a poor public. The clowns take the floor between numbers and speak loudly. They shout, they gesticulate, they lose their balance. They speak into the void. There aren't many people on the bleachers. The audience is bored. They're waiting for the trapeze artists, they want to see a trapeze artist's skeleton shatter on the sawdust-covered ground. They're waiting for the tamer, they want to witness an accident with the bears, they want a bear to tear an arm off the tamer or his daughter. They're not amused by the clowns. No one's laughing. I laugh, but that's because I'm not . . . because I'm different . . . I laugh, but no one else does."

The commentator continues her short speech. She does it softly, but all the same everyone would like her to wrap it up, to put the mic down and bring the music back. It's a live radio broadcast. On the other end, the commentator is facing the public, and the public appreciates her banter, her flattery, the public smiles loudly or applauds when she wants them to. She is like an animal tamer, the obedient audience grovels before her voice and desires to show that they're under her spell. She finally shuts up, the audience applauds once more, and there is a blank in the broadcast, perhaps because the musicians left the stage and have been sitting down. At the same moment, during the blank, a Buddhist voice can be heard.

"You hear that, Yasar?" says Freek. "A religious service on the other side of the wall."

"Yes," says Yasar. "It's coming from next door. It was a dilapidated garage. Old car doors, grimy motors, cans of oil. Red Bonnets converted it into a temple. We have an adjoining wall. It was already thin, but with the renovation work I think it's gotten even thinner. Some days you can hear everything. On top of that we share an air vent. Noises pass through it."

"They're about to begin a ceremony for the deceased. A lama is going to read the *Book of the Dead*. He's going to speak to someone who died recently. He's going to give them advice to help them not be reborn as an animal."

"So you're a religious expert now, Freek?"

"Not really, no . . ."

They listen to the noises coming from the temple. Not much can be heard, actually. A solemn voice, now and then. Not much. Now, the Korean music has returned, a very long piece with syncopated drums and a magnificent soprano voice. Since the radio's sound is very low, not much can be heard from over there, either.

"It's sad," says Yasar after several dull seconds, "thinking about clowns who can't make anyone laugh."

"Out of everyone on the bleachers, I was the only one who did," says Freek. "The spectators watching looked like they didn't understand a thing. Even the children's eyes were blank. They barely reacted at all. I was the only one who found them funny. Maybe it's because I'm not a person. Well, I mean, not a real person . . ."

"Hey, Freek! What are you talking about? Of course you're a person. This isn't because you . . ."

The bartender doesn't continue. He doesn't feel like getting mired down in unsettling considerations, he doesn't want to think aloud about what parts of humanity Freek is lacking. Yasar the bartender's culture has always been resistant to racism, he has always refused to give in to atavistic urges to reject the Other, he has never felt the need to classify Freek in a disparaging animal category, himself being considered a sort of Untermensch, but he prefers not to think about those things aloud in front of Freek. He turns back toward the percolator, he wipes the wall, he rummages through the basket of cutlery.

"Of course you're a real person," he repeats.

A car passes by, the windows tremble in their frame. The lamas' voices come through the partition. A second car passes by, the driver accelerates, he strains his motor without changing speed, the windows shake.

The door opens. A client enters, not a regular: someone unknown, short in stature, dressed like a Sunday proletarian, with a full jacket too long in the sleeves. He has gray hair, a worn-out expression that the lack of sleep has rendered cartoonish.

"Good evening, gentlemen," he says.

His voice lacks confidence.

He goes to sit at a table under a fluorescent light, three meters away from the counter. Freek and Yasar greet him, but don't look at him, Yasar out of professional tact, Freek out of shyness.

"You wouldn't happen to have any salted buttermilk tea, would you?" the newcomer asks.

"No," says Yasar. "We don't have that here."

"I was joking," the man explains.

"Oh," says Yasar.

"Two whiskeys," says the man.

"A double?"

"No. In two glasses. Two doubles. With very few ice cubes."

Yasar disappears the dishcloth he had on his shoulder and gets to work. No one says a word. There's the sound of falling ice cubes, pouring alcohol, the temple bell, the radio. The pansori singer can be heard. Yasar places the glasses on a platter, and brings them to the small man's table. Then he takes his place back in front of Freek. For twenty seconds, they don't speak, both of them, as if the presence of a client behind them is preventing them from picking back up the interrupted conversation. Then Yasar shakes his head.

"You know, Freek," he says. "In my opinion, they're exploiting you, over at the zoo. They know very well that you're going there after hours and taking care of the animals. What you're doing is still work. Night work. They should compensate you."

"Oh, I do it for the animals, not to get dollars," says Freek. "And anyway, they pay me. Some days the director makes me come into his office. He talks to me. He gives me papers to sign. I sign them with my name. He gives me free meal tickets for the watchmen's canteen."

"There's no way they count all your hours," says Yasar. "I'm sure they're exploiting you, Freek."

"No, they do me right. Of course, sometimes . . ."

"Sometimes what?"

"Oh, nothing . . ."

"You were going to say something, Freek."

"No."

"Something that bothers you."

"Well, sometimes they mistake me for an animal," says Freek. "The watchmen. It's an accident, I think. Not out of malice. They grab me on one of the paths before opening time. They don't listen when I protest, like I'm talking to deaf people. No matter how loudly I complain, they open an empty cage and close it again with a padlock. Next to me they put cold food and some straw for toilet paper. There's a sign hung from the bars: PLEASE DON'T FEED THE ANIMALS. While the zoo's open to the public, I keep away from the sign so people don't think it's talking about me. At any rate, I don't get much. The guards leave me there for three or four days. Then, they free me. They apologize. They say it was a truly regrettable mistake, that they accidentally got me confused, and it wasn't out of malice. They say that I look too much like an animal. That they weren't paying attention, because I'm tame, and I talk instead of biting or scratching . . . You see, Yasar? I'd have to bite them for them to see that I'm something other than . . . With all that, Yasar, how should I know that I'm really a person?"

"Stop, Freek," the bartender says. "You're like us, like everyone. Half human, half animal. Everyone's the same way. You, me . . . I can't guarantee I'm a hundred percent human either. I just don't know."

"All the same. No one accidentally throws you in cages, I take it? With hippopotamuses and parrots?"

"Oh, I . . . I was locked up in a special prison for twenty-five years . . . With men and women who'd shot soldiers, ministers . . ."

"Who did you shoot, Yasar?"

"Gangsters."

Yasar was immersed in a hard silence. He'd killed mafiosos, in the past, but only a small number of them, and the species still hadn't disappeared. To the contrary, it had multiplied, reducing other species' territories, polluting other species' daily lives and even their dreams. Yasar floats wordlessly, momentarily in the depths of this failure. The others, Freek and the whiskey drinker, ruminate on what they have said or heard.

A truck rumbles on the boulevard. The windows, and even a few glasses on the shelf behind Yasar, vibrate.

Behind the wall ascend mantras, prayers.

In the radio's disappointing loudspeaker, barely audible since Yasar lowered the sound for reasons unknown, the Korean singer expresses the pain of desertion, the pain of scorned fidelity, the pain of betrayed filial devotion. She has taken on a quavering, but powerful, intonation. It is possible that its unbearable beauty is why the bartender, without thinking, changed the volume.

The small man sitting behind Freek swallows the last mouthful of his first glass.

"You work at the zoo?" he suddenly asks Freek.

Freek turns toward him. His heart always races when a stranger talks to him. Any sort of direct question agonizes him, he feels like trouble must follow. He fears what humans may think, not necessarily their actual threats, but what they might imagine, their cruel and shameful daydreams, often unconfessed, their unconscious depictions of his suffering or death. He pivots frankly toward the stranger and tries to answer naturally, but he can't hide the abrupt pallor of his cheeks, nor the nervous quivering of his eyelids, his lips.

"Yes," he says. "I go to the zoo. I get in through openings in the bars. When the visitors are gone, I talk to the animals. They'd like to be somewhere else. They'd like not to have to die in order to be somewhere else. They shiver in a corner for hours, without stopping. I wait for dusk, I sit near them and speak to them. The animals listen to me. They listen all night through the night, with their ears and muzzles. I try to talk to them until their fear fades away."

The small, worn-out man stirs the ice cubes in his empty glass, then puts it back down in front of him.

"It's not just animals," he says. "I'm in a funk myself. Once you're aware you're trapped in life without any way to get out . . . And then, when you think about those who did get out . . . When you imagine what happens to them after . . . At this very moment, for example . . ."

He attacks his second double whiskey.

"And do you know how to get rid of humans' fears?" he continues.

"No," says Freek. "Not humans. For that, you have to go to a lama."

He clears his throat. He successfully talked with the stranger, but the effort hurt his vocal cords. Now he figures he can end the dialogue without offending the other man. He turns toward Yasar, toward the shelves lined with multicolored bottles.

"Can you make me another caffeine, Yasar?" he says. "I'm going to drink one more bowl and then go. The animals are miserable. It'll be a difficult night for them. I have to leave. They're whining in the darkness, they're waiting for me. They're going to need me. They're terrorized by death. Like the yak. Like the clown."

"Hey!" exclaims the Sunday-dressed proletarian. "How did you know I'm a clown?"

He lifts his arm, an arm with a too-long sleeve, in the half-theatrical gesture of a man who has been drinking.

"Oh, you're a clown?" asks Freek.

"Yes," says the man.

He puts his hand back on the table.

Yasar is once again busying himself with the percolator.

A lama's indecipherable voice wends through the air vent.

"I went to the circus the other day," Freek says. "There were two clowns, Blumschi and Grümscher. One small and one big. They blindly greeted each other from different ends of the floor. Then they ran at each other, they crossed paths but didn't touch. They often fell down."

He pauses to thank Yasar, who's given him a piping black bowl. He leans over it, he breathes. He skims the liquid with his lips to test the temperature. He doesn't risk inhaling it in. He breathes again so that the temperature will drop. It doesn't drop.

"When the big one fell down," continues Freek, "the little one would stop running and rush to help him get back up, but it didn't work. The big one struggled and shouted. It was very funny. He struggled, he refused the little one's help, and he fell back down. It was very comical. But no one laughed, except me. One of the two is dead. I heard some watchmen say he killed himself. He must have been part of a lamaist group. His body was given to the vultures earlier, to the condors, the eagles. Sky burials, they're called. They go into the raptor cage and throw pieces of the body at them. I didn't get near. I was busy talking to the yak. I couldn't see if it was the little one or the big one."

"It was the big one," says the man as he takes a drink of alcohol. "It was Big Grümscher."

"You're sure?" Yasar asks, leaning on the counter.

"Why would I lie to you?" says the man as he swallows another mouthful. "I'm Blumschi, his partner. We worked together at the Schmühl Circus. You must have seen the posters, Schmühl himself put them up in noticeable places, near stoplights, at the entrances to parking lots. Posters with our names on them. Big Grümscher and Little Blumschi, the kings of laughter."

He drinks.

"The kings of laughter," he repeats. "Inseparable. Together forever. More than partners, actually. Much more. Inseparable brothers. And now . . . Now, like the dead once they've passed to the other side, I must go on alone. It's so frightening . . . going alone . . . So painful . . . Grümscher! Can you hear me, Grümscher? How am I going to do it now, all alone, with an unlaughing audience?"

A sob rattles him from head to toe.

"Grümscher!" he says.

"You're a weepy drunk," Yasar observes.

"Not really," says the clown.

"You probably shouldn't finish your second glass," Yasar insists.

"I'm drinking to Grümscher's health," explains Blumschi. "In the temple, they're reading him the *Book of the Dead*, right now. Shaven-skulled bonzes. They do that. And I'm drinking in memory of Big Grümscher."

"It's helpful to read the *Book of the Dead*," Freek intervenes. "Where he is, he's really very alone. He needs someone to reassure him and tell him what to do. You know, if he can hear a voice, even if he can't understand it, he'll feel relieved. He'll be less afraid. Even if it's not true, it'll give him the feeling he's not entirely alone. You should speak to him, instead of drowning yourself in whiskey."

"What do you want me to . . ." says the clown.

His eyes open wide. He looks both drunk and anxious.

"Wait, wait, what are you saying?" he asks.

"He's saying that you should call it quits on the whiskey," says the bartender.

"I'm saying that it would do him good to hear your voice right now," says Freek. "He's just beginning. It's very difficult, at the start. It'll have an effect on him. He may not recognize your voice right away. But it'll do him good."

"I don't know how to talk to a dead person," says the clown. "I've never had the chance to . . . And anyway, have you really thought about what it means to talk to a dead man? Thinking he can hear you? That he's listening to you, from his dark world, from . . . It's frightening . . . And if he misinterprets what you're trying to . . . Did you think about that? If, instead of reassuring him, you end up terrorizing him? No, I really don't see what I could . . ."

"You only have to do what you were doing onstage," Freek suggests. "When he was struggling, when you yelled advice in his ear to help him get back up and he pretended not to hear you."

"Or else, you only have to murmur phrases from the *Book of the Dead*," says Yasar. "Reassuring formulas."

"For what I know of the *Book of the Dead*'s formulas . . ." Blumschi protests. "Big Grümscher could have . . . he could recite entire pages by heart. He loved Buddhist magic, he was a member of a mutual aid group that read the *Book of the Dead* to those suffering in the streets, to vagrants, to the tatterdemalion . . . He took courses at the lamaist school. We were inseparable, but that put a chasm between us. I've never . . . I'm completely incapable of . . ."

"They're reading it next door," says Freek. "You only have to listen to a passage and repeat it."

Blumschi drinks. He doesn't retort. He puts his glass back down. Under the ice cubes, the liquid is transparent. If my count is correct, he's just finished his fourth whiskey.

There is still the background noise of the radio in the bar, along with the diverse ringings and murmurs coming from the Buddhist ceremony on the other side of the wall. The officiant's voice is distorted by the path it had to travel before arriving behind the counter. It is however a minimal distance, with negligible obstacles, a few bricks, a square of fine wire mesh. It's a mystery what the dead man can perceive of this voice, being an incalculable distance away.

"You can't distinguish anything, anyway," Blumschi complains. "Not a syllable."

"I'm going to turn off the radio," Yasar proposes. "I can also undo the grill on the vent duct. They put the temple in the old service station next door. The vents to the bar and the garage are connected. We'll hear everything."

"Great," says Blumschi.

He pushes his chair back. He rises. He is drunk.

"Well," he says. "One last drop to your health, my old Grümscher. And then, you're going to see how I communicate with the garage and you."

He grabs his glass, he examines the ice cubes which offer him nothing more than poorly flavored water. He staggers. He collides with a table.

The bartender turns off the radio. Then he climbs on a stool, loosens something behind the bottle shelves, above the bar's partition. Suddenly, the sounds coming from the neighboring building transform. It feels like they are right in the heart of the temple. The lama's profound bass resonates inside the bar as if the lama was standing behind the counter, between the percolator and Yasar.

"Oh noble son," says the lama, "I am once again going to repeat this first page of the *Bardo Thödol*, so important it is for you to hear and to understand, without which you will be lost for the forty-nine days of your journey through the Bardo."

"Well?" says the bartender. "Don't tell me you still can't distinguish the syllables. It's quite stunning, isn't it? Go on, Blumschi, you don't have any more excuses. Have faith! Repeat everything to your friend."

"Pour me another whiskey," Blumschi says, panicking. "I . . . This feels obscene. I'm not drunk enough for public speaking."

Yasar hesitates for a second, then he stretches his hand toward the bottle. He prepares the drink Blumschi requires.

"He needs guidance," says Freek. "Don't make anything up, give him the same advice the monks do. Let yourself guide him through what the monks say. The most important thing is for him to recognize your voice. Your voice and your way of speaking. He has to know that his friend is still nearby to help him. It will do him immense good. It will help him not drown completely in terror."

"Oh noble son, Grümscher," the lama says, "I am addressing you as I will every day for forty-nine days. It is absolutely necessary that you lend me your ear and do your best to understand the meaning of my words. What I am telling you now is meant to ease your crossing of the Bardo. If you listen to me without distraction, you will be less afraid when you are walking the Bardo's dreadful, narrow passages. You will even be able to escape the disastrous prospect of endless rebirth and death, and rebirth again, and death again. You will be able to liberate yourself from this long chain of suffering."

The small clown takes hold of the glass Yasar filled. He swallows several mouthfuls with glum anxiety.

"Put your glass down, Blumschi," says Yasar.

"Yes," says Blumschi as he wobbles, not putting his glass down.

"Talk to your friend," says Yasar. "Everything is strange and unpleasant to him right now. If that's the case, he won't even realize he's not alive anymore. He doesn't know how to react at all. Talk to him so he knows that a friend is trying to help him."

"It's obscene," says Blumschi.

"Go on," Yasar encourages him. "It's not obscene. It's a moment of very strong friendship. Pretend like you're together again on the circus floor, before the public. Like obscenity doesn't exist."

"Before the public . . ." Blumschi grumbles as he staggers. "Like . . ."

Then he overcomes his reluctance and launches into it. He moves his arms and pretends to flap between the first tables and the counter. In his pauper's clothes, held together with four safety pins, he is grotesque, but that's precisely what he's going for. In an instant he has become a clownish character who makes no one laugh. He widens his despair-laden eyes and grimaces dazedly, and now he is raising his pitch, whining in an acute voice.

"Can Big Grümscher hear me?" he bawls. "Does he hear Little Blumschi? Yes? No? Where is Big Grümscher? Has anyone seen him, perchance? Where is Big Grümscher hiding? Oh oh oh! He wouldn't happen to be hiding in a big, big vulture's big, big gizzard, would he? Or on the crematorium's big, hot grill? Where could Big Grümscher be hiding? In the Bardo? Could Big Grümscher have gone and hid in the Bardo?"

A car passes by. The windows clink. Blumschi takes a drink. He puts his glass down on the counter with an imprecise gesture.

"It's useless," he says. "I'm sure he can't hear me. Even if he could, it'd just be a bigger nightmare."

"What would?" asks Freek.

"If my voice reached him," says Blumschi.

There are two seconds of silence.

"Oh noble son, Grümscher," says the lama, "you have remained unconscious for several days. When you left this void, you asked yourself: 'What happened? What has come about?' . . . You try to consult your memories, but everything is hazy in your mind. You have trouble recognizing the world around you."

"Go on," says Yasar. "Continue, Blumschi. Too bad if it's a nightmare. It's for his own good."

The clown opens his eyes wide. They are damp with tears. He makes a ridiculous, exaggerated grimace, but his expression betrays an immense sorrow.

"Does Big Grümscher hear me?" he bawls. "Does the big buffoon hear me or not? Well? Has he had enough of being unconscious? He opens his eyes, and what does he see? The acrobats' crossbar, where the big straw mats sway when they're hung up, that's what he sees! And he consults his memories, and what does Big Grümscher say? 'What's come about?' he says! 'What happened? And why is Little Blumschi all shook up, why is he crying and blowing his nose so loudly?'"

The clown gesticulates. He spins around, stretching out his arms, like a shaman on the brink of a trance, though it is obvious he hardly believes in the spectacle's worth. On top of that, his gestures are uncertain. With the back of the hand, he slaps the platter Yasar had used to serve his whiskies. The glasses go flying, a saucer rolls off, everything shatters on the ground.

"Oh, blasted yak rot! I broke your dishes," he says, doubtlessly relieved to have found a pretext for taking a break.

"It's nothing," says Yasar. "I'll clean it up. Don't stop."

"You are having difficulty deciphering the universe which has welcomed you," continues the lama. "You understand nothing. Nothing is familiar to you. Without an effort on your part, you are going to be as ill-equipped to interpret the post-death world as a baby in the post-birth world. React, noble son. Do not let yourself become submerged in dread. Do not imagine either that you are finally walking into reality. Everything around you is just another illusion. Do not become attached to this illusion, as deceitful and vain as the existence you just left."

"You're acting like Big Grümscher was attached to this existence," Blumschi remarks.

He picks up a piece of glass from the ground. Tears run down his cheeks.

"Leave it," says Yasar.

Blumschi gets back up. He didn't even have time to cut his palm. He is standing in the small puddle, surrounded by nearly-melted ice cubes, alive, not even wounded. He is comical. No one feels like laughing.

"Do not become at all attached to it," says the lama.

"Is Big Grümscher still listening?" Little Blumschi suddenly continues. "Does he hear Mister Lama, huh? Is he listening to Mister Lama? Is he not letting himself become submerged in dread? Is floating in vultures' gastric juices not doing anything for him? Oh, but I heard that the Grümscher is a little afraid . . . Don't be afraid, you big straw mat! It's for a laugh! It's just an unreal world! It's a silly illusion! You have to get used to it, Big Grümscher! Don't get attached!"

Sobs suffocate Little Blumschi. A truck passes by. The windows tremble. Blumschi has slumped into a chair to cry.

"I can't," says the clown. "It's too absurd. It's making everyone suffer."

"Don't stop, Blumschi," says Freek. "Don't cry too loudly. You don't want him to hear you crying. Keep helping him like you were. The big one's afraid. He's woken up and is afraid. It does him an enormous good to hear you. Don't stop shouting your inanities. I'm sure it's doing him an enormous good."

"Who cares about my inanities?" says Blumschi. "He can't hear me."

Blumschi sniffles. He sits up straight in his chair. He listens to the religious man's voice describing the best attitudes for the dead man to adopt should any problems arise, but now the discourse is in a ritual Tibetan which the least useful intonation no one in the bar can glean.

"You never know," says Freek. "But maybe, down there, in the dark, he understood. He wanted to laugh in the dark. Maybe. He was afraid, then he was less afraid."

"Poor guy," says Blumschi. "He didn't laugh for months at a time. He was drowning in depression and couldn't get out. Nobody found us funny anymore. Big Grümscher was a great clown though. I'm not saying that just to indulge him, or because I loved him like a brother. I'm saying it because it's true. He was a consummate professional. But we still couldn't get any laughs from the bleachers anymore. Sympathetic murmurs, yes, two or three snickers, but no laughs. Big Grümscher started to feel like it was too much, in the circus, in life. He felt completely useless. Nothing helped convince him to the contrary. In the last few days he was dwelling down there for good. He was convinced he was lost in an awful dream."

Yasar sweeps the glass fragments, the ice cubes. He makes the puddle disappear. He thinks about Blumschi, about Grümscher, about Freek. He recalls the years in captivity, he reflects on the strange pointlessness of existence, no matter what anyone wants. He rinses the ground under the table, he takes the mop near the counter. We all feel like we are lost inside an awful dream, and, if you add together all the insignificant moments of the present, the dream carries on.

"You know," Blumschi says, "when a clown can't make anyone laugh, he can go mad with grief. You go onstage, the projectors blind you, it's freezing cold, the circus reeks of old beasts, the smell of piss rises from the sand, and you're there, to thrash around, to shout, like you're extremely lonely, with the hope that, despite everything, someone on the bleachers will soon start laughing, in the darkness you can hardly see because of the lamps. But no one flinches. No one giggles or roars. And it's unbearable. It drives you mad. Years like that, living it night after night. Waiting for laughs that never come."

"You made me laugh," says Freek. "I went to see you at the Schmühl Circus. I saw both of you. The kings of laughter, like on the poster. I was in the dark, on the bleachers. The third row. There were some children. They had stopped talking. The closest ones were annoyed that I was sitting next to them. They tried to move away. I didn't dare laugh out loud once I realized that I was the only one who found you funny. But I had a stomachache. You made me laugh. I don't think I've ever laughed so much in my life."

"Yes, but with you, it's not the same," says Blumschi. "You're not really . . . I mean . . ."

Freek jabs his nose into his bowl of caffeine. He still had the bottom to finish.

"Each one of us is mired in his own awful dream," the clown says. "You're there, petrified with grief on top of the stinking sand, and, as petrified as you are, you keep struggling, emitting sounds . . . You wait for a friendly laugh to echo from the dark. You wait for a friendly voice to encourage you, agree with you, pull you from there . . . And nothing. Nothing comes . . . The darkness remains silent. You do the best clownings in your repertoire, and the children move away. No bursts of laughter . . . So you don't even believe in friendship anymore. You move away yourself. You close up. You don't even try sharing your grief with Little Blumschi. You go hang around under the acrobats' crossbar one night. You go hang around under the acrobats' crossbar one night, and you hang yourself."

Blumschi is once again slumped in his chair. He spoke those last sentences in a broken voice. Mucus and tears soil his cheeks.

Yasar rinsed the mop in the bucket, then he washed Freek's bowl, some saucers, a spoon. At one point, he closed the air vent connected to the temple. The reading of the *Bardo Thödol* became a distant, uninterpretable murmur. Grümscher can perhaps be heard better right now in his mysterious darkness, but the lama's guidance is unintelligible.

A police car races down the boulevard. The revolving lights color a wall red and blue for a second. The windows quiver.

Freek has left for the zoo.

Yasar turns the radio back on. It's the Korean music program again. For those in the know, it is now a traditional dance, accompanied by a popular oboist, the *hyangpiri*, an hourglass-shaped drum, the *changgo*, a cylindrical drum, the *puk*, and flutes. For others, it's just lovely music that can be listened to for hours, because it's rhythmic, because it's beautiful, and because they are extremely lonely.

Antoine Volodine is the primary pseudonym of a French writer who has published twenty books under this name, several of which are available in English translation, including *Post-Exoticism in Ten Lessons, Lesson Eleven* (also available from Open Letter) and *Minor Angels*. He also publishes under the names Lutz Bassmann (*We Monks & Soldiers*) and Manuela Draeger (*In the Time of the Blue Ball*). Most of his works take place in a post-apocalyptic world where members of the "post-exoticism" writing movement have all been arrested as subversive elements. Together, these works constitute one of the most inventive, ambitious projects of contemporary writing.

J.T. Mahany is a graduate of the masters program in literary translation at the University of Rochester and is currently enrolled in the MFA program at the University of Arkansas. He is also the translator of *Post-Exoticism in Ten Lessons, Lesson Eleven* by Antoine Volodine.

Open Letter—the University of Rochester's nonprofit, literary translation press—is one of only a handful of publishing houses dedicated to increasing access to world literature for English readers. Publishing ten titles in translation each year, Open Letter searches for works that are extraordinary and influential, works that we hope will become the classics of tomorrow.

Making world literature available in English is crucial to opening our cultural borders, and its availability plays a vital role in maintaining a healthy and vibrant book culture. Open Letter strives to cultivate an audience for these works by helping readers discover imaginative, stunning works of fiction and poetry, and by creating a constellation of international writing that is engaging, stimulating, and enduring.

Current and forthcoming titles from Open Letter include works from Argentina, Catalonia, China, Iceland, Israel, Latvia, Poland, Spain, South Africa, and many other countries.

www.openletterbooks.org

2x ¹⁰/₁₆ (⁷/₁₇)
2x 10/16 (12/22)

WITHDRAWN
FROM THE COLLECTION OF
THE BRYANT LIBRARY